NOBODY'S PATRIOT

by
Harvey Green

dragon
tree books

1620 SW 5th Avenue
Pompano Beach, Florida 33060
(954)788-4775
editors@editingforauthors.com
dragontreebooks.com

To my wife Judy, without her encouragement, inspiration, and support, this book would would not exist.

To my parents Gene and Mary Katherine, who gave me the mental capacity to to never quit.

And to my children Harvey and Raychel, whom I love dearly, and because you both have your feet planted firmly on earth you never needed to pull me away from my writing to bale you out.

And to Todd Brock for dragging me into all this.

To my readers, thank you all for your interest in my work, I hope you enjoy this story.

CONTENTS

PROLOGUE

*I*t was Friday, the 21st of May 2010, and Harry had just settled back in his desk chair from an early lunch when his cellphone went off. Todd Brock's name appeared on the screen. Harry was Todd's new neighbor, two doors to the west of his own recently purchased home on Southampton Circle. Harry and Todd had met a few months earlier at The Mermaid one afternoon while sitting side by side at the bar. The Mermaid, a quaint lakeside neighborhood restaurant and bar just down the street was a convenient but upscale gathering place for locals. Having similar occupational backgrounds, they'd hit it off quickly as they talked about crappie and bass fishing in the lake. Harry had learned that Todd was a project executive with a well-known construction firm—a position much like his own in his former life.

He answered the phone. "What's up, bud?"

"Harry, you know that house you were talking about buying, over here by me in Lake Caroline? Well, they're shooting it up like crazy right now.

"Say what?" he screeched. "I've already bought the house, and that guy is renting it back for a month."

"Well ol' Calvin Singer, the guy you bought it from, apparently lost his marbles at the clinic today and has gotten into a standoff with your buddy Eddie "Bluelite"; you might want to get out there. I just left my house, and the sheriff was barricading the streets and running everybody outta there, hell you might not even be able to get in."

Harry wasn't much for analyzing the criminal mind; as far as he was concerned, that was for eggheads in Langley and Washington to work through, fodder for some Ph.D. candidate's hack-job dissertation. Pushing the speed limit to get out to Lake Caroline, Harry worried that he'd never see his new home or the seller again. He couldn't help but feel like he should have seen this coming.

Harry arrived at the subdivision entry boulevard, and though it was visibly intended to be blocked with "Police Line Do Not Cross" tape, since it was tied between two squad cars, he saw that he could easily pass around the barrier on the grassy shoulder. He could see that all the law enforcement and onlookers had gotten out of their cars and walked down to where the action was, as though there was a parade or fireworks show about to begin. Harry knew, or thought he knew, what was going on up there and figured since he owned the house and knew a little about it, maybe they would excuse his interference into an active police scene. As he drove his pickup around and past the barricade, he thought, *fireworks show all right,* one that the onlookers might not be prepared for. As he passed by several empty squad cars, two news vans and a host of military-looking guys in body armor each holding M4 carbines, he couldn't believe that he made it this far in without getting stopped, but no one seemed to care, all eyes were focused on what was going on over the hill at Harry's house.

He coasted his pickup as quietly as he could near a barrel-chested deputy holding a bullhorn and a deep frown. The only thing that concerned Harry was getting Calvin Singer, the former homeowner turned short-term renter, out of the house without blowing the place to smithereens.

Throwing it into park, the automatic door locks popped open as he reached for the ignition key: He cut the engine and gradually exited his pickup, doing his best to appear to be someone who belonged in the area rather than some curious passer-by. Even though it was a couple blocks over from his house, he could tell that it was a tense situation, so Harry took his time walking toward the deputy. The way he saw it, Cal likely wasn't going anywhere.

When he had bought the place on Southampton Circle in Lake Caroline, he had sort of expected there to be complications. It was a fairly new house in a fledgling fairly new subdivision, which usually meant nosy neighbors, first-time homeowners, and retirees eager to protect their not so insignificant investments. As usual, everyone wanted to hold court over who was moving in and what kind of neighbor he or she might be, as though they could somehow prevent it if they had a mind to.

Harry pondered his house from the distance; he could not see over the hill and around the curve to Southampton but he had sized them up in his mind; it had been plain as the nose on his face that this couple was a little different. Decorating was not what he would have expected, the seller's wife had more than likely done their own decorating, which meant pale pink walls, large ornate picture frames and oversized chandeliers. Calvin had overseen the tasteless overgrown landscaping across the front yard, probably under his wife's direction, as no one would hardly pay a price for what was there.

There was no doubt that Harry would have to invest time and money into it to get the place back up to the grandeur and high standards of the surrounding homes as well as the entire neighborhood, which to him really wasn't an issue pricewise, seeing as it would all be done on the Company's dime, but it would also mean a move-in delay and spending a whole bunch of time sweeping down the place, he had no idea what all Calvin may have hidden in the walls, the attic and even the floor.

Calvin had seemed like an ordinary guy all right and okay with the sell, albeit he was always a bit edgy and he drank far too much for Harry's taste. What Harry did not expect was for Cal to go berserk and hole himself up in there with enough guns and ammo to stand off the Mexicans at the Alamo.

The anchors on WTFN speculated, half-joking, that the weather must have had something to do with it. "It's an unseasonably warm day," they said, "It's been a bizarrely hot spring; not much rain, hot every day for over a month. We've had eight days in a row over ninety. That's pretty warm for early May in Mississippi."

Statistics proved that violent crime went up along with the mercury, but while it was indeed a hot day, it was hardly a prolonged heat wave. Harry, recalling what he'd seen while touring the house with the Realtor, and he had other ideas of what was behind Cal's siege. Post-traumatic stress disorder (PTSD) was more likely or money—the lack of it. Maybe even wife troubles or all three; surely this must be the case with Calvin Singer.

He squinted at the deputy, casting about for his name tag before finding it. "That you, Mark?" he called out.

Deputy Sandridge turned on him, burned pink, sweating with heat and obvious anxiety. "Yeah, it's me. O'Keefe, right? Harry O'Keefe?"

"The one and only, far as I know." Harry walked over to him; hand outstretched.

Deputy Sandridge's hand was as soaked as his brow. "Well, I'll be damned—what are you doing out here; you know you weren't supposed to cross that police line back there, right? Wait, don't tell me this is your place the crazy bastard's holed up in? Your buddy in there just let out a hailstorm of bullets."

"He ain't my buddy. I bought the place from him six weeks ago, rented it back to him for about a month; he was supposed to be moving out today. I got a call from Todd Brock telling me about what was going on out here."

"We knew this guy had some fancy stuff in there, all legally acquired, no less. We saw the permits come through, but for a guy with that many weapons, he ain't much of a shot, thank goodness. The poor bastard must have snapped and lost it, decided the best and most sensible course of action was to shoot a patient and the receptionist at his therapist's office, then speed home and spend all afternoon trading fire with Madison County sheriff's deputies."

Harry, twisting his neck a bit, gave a dry chuckle. "If you're waiting for him to run out of ammo, I'd suggest calling up The Mermaid and getting your standoff catered; from what I saw he could burn Dupont and lead for hours, he's got enough in there to fight a small war."

"Well, he found one, I'll tell ya that."

Sandridge and other deputies had positioned themselves further from the house and had set up a command center at the boulevard roundabout, a few blocks away from Southampton Circle, so that they could divert homeowner traffic and rubberneckers away from the danger zone.

Normally on this day of the year, everyone out there would have had their focus on the annual catfish tournament set to begin that evening, but considering what was going on at Harry's place, the fishermen preferred to watch that spectacle from a distance, eating hamburgers and chugging cold beers—sort of a tailgate party on their anchored pontoon boats. The Mermaid had taken on a brisk early-evening business of selling beer and burgers to all the spectators. It was probably their best night that week—standing room only on the front porch.

Harry recognized Chief Eddie Belvedresi's voice squelching through the radio clipped to Sandridge's shoulder, "I see several more residents standing outside their front doors trying to see what's going on over here, I need more officers to canvas the houses from the golf-course side and get all of these people out of here before a stray bullet kills one of them."

A news helicopter hovered a few hundred feet overhead and an eighteen-wheeler hauling an old Vietnam Era armored personnel carrier was working his way around the command post headed to the house on Southampton Circle. The loud noise was canceling out all conversation, forcing Sandridge to yell into the radio. "I got you covered, Chief. I'm sending Tackett and Logan around by the golf course with a bullhorn; they'll get it done."

The street in front of Harry's place was covered in shell casings; every officer there had emptied as least one magazine from their service Glock. Now shielding themselves behind their police cruiser, each had their own automatic rifles trained on the front door of the residence. An hour earlier, the suspect had been seen loading his Hummer with rifles and ammunition in preparation for what the chief later said was likely an evil plan to return to the clinic and kill everyone there.

The chief had received a call from headquarters to go and arrest the guy at 109 Southampton Circle, approach in reduced code but expedite, suspect's name is Calvin Singer and may be armed. Suspect is traveling in a gold colored Hummer, late model, license plate MA1-9546.

Chief Belvidresi lived in the same neighborhood just a few blocks away and had just finished his lunch a home. He quickly drove to the address on Southampton Circle but he couldn't help it, the hair on his neck was sticking up like a bad haircut. Along the way he'd begun to have a sinking spell about this one. *Could this be a bad one*, he thought, *after all these years, was this going to be the one that went all wrong; just what I need today. And wasn't this the street that his friend Harry had recently purchased a house on, he sure hoped it wasn't.* He developed a lump in his throat as he whipped his black slick-top into the driveway of the residence; there stood his suspect with an arm full of long guns.

"Hey fellow, hold up for sec, I need to talk to you" the chief said in a low and calm voice from the window of his unit. Cal gave him a cold stare as he retreated into his house inside the garage, hurriedly returning with another arm load of weapons. Belvedresi knew this look, he had seen it too many times and to him, this was not going to end on a good note. Once again he spoke, "Hey fellow, wait up a minute … we need to talk." His voice a bit more stern at this point but his demand was returned with another glassy-eyed stare, as if red laser beams were emitting from his eyes straight to Eddie's eyes. Cal returned to the house a second time, minutes later as just Chief Belvidresi was about to exit his vehicle, Calvin emerged in full battle gear, helmet, flak jacket and all; wielding an M-16 fully automatic rifle, he began firing, fanning from side to side, spraying bullets in every direction. The chief took cover behind the driver's side door of his cruiser, slamming it in reverse simultaneously returning fire along with 4 other deputies that had now arrived at the scene. A bullet pierced Cal's left wrist, a critical wound but Calvin managed to retreat through the kitchen door off the garage using the Hummer as a shield. A critical wound but Calvin managed to retreat through the kitchen door off the garage using the Hummer as a shield. The door snapped locked as Cal made it through.

Attempts to contact Calvin via cellphone had all gone to voicemail, and no movement was seen through the windows. The Chief repeatedly tried for the next hour to try to coax Calvin out by bullhorn, but Cal remained silent and hidden somewhere in the house.

Another hour had passed, just then a gun barrel poked out the living room window and spat a stream of rounds at an adjacent squad car, breaking the side glass out.

Harry squatted with the sound even though he was more than three blocks away and not in direct site of the house; he duck-walked over to get behind the nearest cruiser, followed closely by Sandridge.

"Son of a bitch," Sandridge said as his radio crackled; a voice came through on the other end.

"Deputy Sandridge, be advised, we're sending additional officers for backup." The clipped, brutish tones of Sheriff Trowbridge cut through the buzzing engines and crack of

gunfire. "I've got the governor standing by and he is willing to send the goddamn National Guard in there if we need them; you just give the word."

Another voice came in over Sandridge's Motorola. "You might want to go ahead and put your backup on red alert; this son of a bitch is bound and determined to kill somebody, and he's not looking to come out alive."

Harry's spirits lifted a bit at the second voice. "That Bluelite?" he asked. "Tell him O'Keefe is here with you and I would like nothing more than not getting my new house blown up—I just bought the thing last month, okay."

Sandridge cued his mic. "Chief, I got Harry O'Keefe here, the new homeowner." He gave a solemn chuckle. "Says he sure would appreciate you using a little resistive willpower on the hand grenades, he doesn't want you to blow his new house up."

"Damn, I knew he had a place over here, sure was hoping this one wasn't it. Well, you tell him I can't make promises, but we'll do the best we can. This guy's nuts." Bluelite wasn't known for taking it easy. "We been out here for three hours; he already shot two of my guys and put two folks back at that clinic in the hospital. We'll get him if we have to drive this armored carrier through the front door to do it. I hope Harry's got some good insurance."

Harry pursed his lips, mouthing a string of cuss words; his old pal Eddie had been bumped up from the highway patrol, where he earned his nickname "Bluelite," affectionately given him by his fellow troopers, owing to his unprecedented string of stops and arrests. Chronic speeders feared him, and drug runners traveled hours out of their way to minimize their time in the Jackson Metro area. He even put a state police officer in cuffs over a DUI at a time when that kind of thing would usually slide.

As chief deputy, he developed a reputation as a tough but fair officer with a great sense of humor. Everything was done by the book, from jaywalking and domestic disturbances all the way up to first-degree murder. He had established good relationships with state and local police alike, and he knew all the local feds by name. He discouraged deadly force among his deputies, while making it clear that if an officer had to pull his or her weapon, the target better not be a threat for much longer. He'd earned every commendation they could give a trooper, held his roto-wing and twin-engine certificates too. He'd served as chief pilot for Mississippi Highway Patrol, even flew the governor around when needed.

But Bluelite got sick of the politics and his best friend, Toby Trowbridge, had already retired and had been elected sheriff of

Madison County. He was going to need a new top-notch chief deputy, if he won. He and Eddie had served together for years on the state force, a man he could trust to get it done. He encouraged Eddie to go ahead and take his retirement, which was overdue as it was; and come work for him. Bluelite took the gig, and that's how the legend wound up overseeing the standoff at Harry's new place.

Harry had grown up in the same rural town of Clarksdale as Eddie; they were friends and ran in the same crowds. Even though he had left the state and gone into a wildly different line of work, he still respected his friend's dogged commitment to getting his man; besides, it never hurt to know a high-ranking lawman when your ass was in a sling. Now, though, he couldn't help but wish Eddie would just loosen up a bit.

"Tell him I'd appreciate a little restraint. I've been through that place a half dozen times; I can give you the layout, let you know what you're dealing with. I know where he keeps his guns and ammo. His wife in there with him?"

Sandridge shook his head, "Negative, she flew the coop. Florida, I think, waiting till this thing is over, I guess." He spoke briefly into his radio then reached into his notebook and tore out a page, handing it over to Harry along with a pen. "Go ahead and draw us a little floor plan of the place; how much equipment does he have in there?"

"Best I can remember, I'd say at least one M-16, two MP5s, an Uzi, a few AR-15s, an AK-47, a Dragunov sniper rifle, a vintage Mosin-Nagant, several tactical pump shotguns, all scoped out, pistols, and plenty of rounds to go with all of them. He's also got a few smoke grenades, flash bangs, and an M203 grenade launcher.

Hell, when I first saw it, I had him pegged for the Army Reserves or the National Guard, with all the equipment he's got in there."

Sandridge let out a low whistle. "What was he expecting, an invasion, a shootout? This ain't the Waco, damn; Eddie wants to know what part of the house you would guess he'd be holed up in, the front or back?"

"Well, most of his stuff is in the office near the garage door leading from the kitchen, but honestly, he has stuff stuck in every closet in the house, front to back."

Harry drew his lips tight, thinking back to his many conversations with Cal. "That's the question, isn't it? The guy was wound tight; I wish I could say I was more surprised."

"Wound tight?" Sandridge replied. "Hell, I come home after a long day of dealing with drug addicts and knife-wielding husbands and idiots that don't believe Hell is hot and all I do is kiss my wife, open a beer, and kick my boots off. I know wound tight, but yeah, I bet he's wound tighter than dick's hatband."

Another flurry of gunfire sent them ducking back behind the cruiser. The SWAT guys returned fire from the rear of the house, off the golf course, launching a couple more tear gas grenades though the glass doors out back, as Cal shouted something unintelligible their way. Harry sighed, the sun was beginning to set, and he realized with every passing minute the chances of his new home going up in smoke increased exponentially. Resigning himself to doing everything he could to bring this to an end as soon as possible, he began to draw out the floor plan of the house with neat, clean lines.

"This is how you'll get him."

One

"**I**'m telling you, man," Matt said through his third single malt. "Russia is the place to be."

Cal nodded at his friend as they sat in The Westward, a dusty bar and grill in downtown Jackson, Mississippi. Cal had wanted to go to a more proper watering hole, like The Mermaid, but Matt had made an ass out of himself and had gotten kicked out of every respectable establishment in the metro area. Early-evening summer light streamed through the windows.

"So, you've said," Cal replied. "I have to be at work at ten tonight; you understand that, right? I already got one strike, don't have time for a whole yarn."

"I don't think you're listening to me. This is no joke, my friend." Matt nodded with half a smile at a divorcée across the bar; she smiled politely and turned away. Matt wasn't much to look at, and his braying Jersey accent didn't help. "My guys over there will give you a job, they need someone with your skillset. Look, you got booze, you got drugs, and the women. Oh my god, the women." He let out a low breath, allowed the air to pass his teeth.

To Cal, this was a wearisome routine; every time his friend came back home, he'd insist on going out and regaling anyone who would listen with tales of the money he earned and the girls he'd had over in Russia. Cal tolerated it on account of not having a whole lot of friends and when Matt was done with all that, the evening usually panned out pretty well.

After all, Calvin Singer had never been much of a socializer and had been basically a loner most all his life. As a young student, it hadn't taken long for teachers and parents alike to realize that despite solid grades, he didn't have the disposition for school; even in the first grade he'd spent almost as much time in front of the principal for fighting as he did in class. For Calvin there wasn't a lot to do in Owensboro, Kentucky, besides mine coal, barbeque mutton, or an occasional beer bust down on the banks of the Ohio River. The restless quiet enabled violence, and young Cal was only too eager to oblige, but today, today, he would bite his tongue and think of his future for just a minute. Besides, maybe Matt was on to something. Cal took another big gulp from his beer mug.

"Look, I understand that you're going to peddle this employer of yours to anyone who will listen," Cal said. "But I'm done with all that. I ain't trying to do nothing but work my shift and drink my beer in peace; Army was enough adventure for a lifetime."

Matt laughed. "You rode a desk for almost all of it."

"Don't forget one whole month in a cell for some shit I didn't even start. Now I'm just trying to do right."

When Cal graduated from high school, college had been nowhere near his consideration. The future held two options for him: jail or the military. So, having lived a life miraculously free of misdemeanors up until that point, he enlisted in the Army.

"You know, I live here too, and street talk is that you are a bit of a tough guy, is that right, is that why you want to join up?" the recruiter had said. "Well no Sir, the thing is, I am just floundering around and need something to get me focused, if you know what I mean. I mean, I figure if I join up maybe I can learn a good skill that will help me find a place to fit in later, you know, make a living and all" "Yes, the Army can help you do that but look, I have to tell you up front, the Army won't tolerate a man that can't control his temper and his manners; this is a professional organization. We protect the Constitution and America by fighting its enemies not each other. Do you understand me, young man?"

Cal just nodded, impressed by the quiet authority of the clean-cut man in front of him; there wasn't anybody like that where he lived.

Basic training absolutely kicked his ass, but it also toughened him up. He loved to pull the trigger, and excelled in hand-to-hand combat but in the end, it was his damn temper that got the best of him. He achieved the rank of Private First Class after 16 months and later applied and became a 17C, Cyber Operations Specialist, stationed at Fort Meade in Maryland. At long last, he'd found his niche.

Before he had served a full 3 years, his record of constant fighting, both on and off base, had finally gotten him brought up on some pretty serious charges. At his court-martial, the judge took the time to impress upon Cal and everyone present that Cal had thrown a promising career away, that for somebody like him, it would likely never get much better than this. It was an act of mercy that he would only spend 30 days in the brig and be "Other than Honorable" discharged.

That is how he wound up sitting at this sticky bar in Jackson, sucking down Coors Light and waiting for his shift as a security guard.

"Do you honestly believe you're reaching your potential? Wandering around an office building all night with a torch, reporting in?" Matt talked into an imaginary radio, his voice nasal. "*All clear by this cubicle....* Meanwhile I'm running around Russia, throwing fifties at nude models; they go wild for American currency, let me tell you. And you should see the clubs over there: disco balls everywhere, bottle service for all. It's like the eighties over there." He chuckled. "They never got the good life under Khrushchev and that drunk Yeltsin bastard—now they're living it up."

Cal gritted his teeth and stared into his warming beer; it was true, with his record, no one wanted to hire him for anything that required more training than a high school diploma or more responsibility than a guard dog. He had wandered around the country, crashing on couches, working as a bouncer, handyman, anything that would pay. He excelled at none of it and was often fired quickly. The bosses would watch him, waiting for the disgraced veteran to slip up and lose his temper before they kicked him to the curb.

Cal felt he was being devoured and then spat back out by a world that didn't understand him. Couldn't they all see it wasn't his fault? He'd been raised with fighting parents in a burned-out coal town. He was a product of his environment, and he couldn't be blamed for his blazing temper and the permanent chip on his shoulder.

"Who do you work for, anyway?" he asked Matt. "You never gave me a name."

Matt smiled and tapped the side of his nose. "That's the best part: it's all legitimate business. These are multimillionaires, billionaires even, no regulation, no SEC to keep them down, just pure business."

"I didn't hear a name. In my experience anyone whose job is 'business' ain't much of a business if you ask me."

"Look, after the Soviet Union fell apart, what were they supposed to do? They sure weren't getting paid back when it was all black bread and toilet vodka. Now it's caviar and champagne every night. Beluga too, not the fish bait they sell in the supermarket here."

For a moment Cal felt some connection to his friend's mysterious bosses; he too couldn't get paid his fair share, hopping from job to job, everywhere from Oregon to Atlanta. Wasn't it hard enough to earn a decent living without a man's sins weighing him down?

But still, it smelled wrong to him, always had. Cal had met Matt through a mutual friend, a drug dealer who claimed to be a mechanic but never seemed to be putting in hours. Matt was a cheap kind of friend, with a wet handshake and beady, darting eyes in his doughy face. A patently distrustful kind of man, and given that Cal had plenty of friends in low places, he knew the type; they only really spent time together so Matt could hold court on various topics and lord his supposed jet-setting lifestyle over the less fortunate.

"Not interested in illegal work," Cal said. "I'm not looking to add to my record."

"Whoa, whoa," Matt held up his arms, stretching the sleeves of his jacket almost to the point of splitting the seams. "This isn't illegal; this is a real Russian industry. My boss is an importer, and there is no reason America and the Russians can't have a good relationship, right? We should be trading with Russia, sharing all our best with each other, else, what's the point, right? That's plain ol' capitalism, the way I see it."

"Why even offer me a job? What's in it for you?"

"Isn't it enough for us to just be buddies? Can I not help a friend out without getting the third degree? Look, my boss needs good people, Americans." Matt searched around for a server. "He needs people who know their way around a computer and have the guts to get things done—that's you, man." He raked the back of his hand across Cal's shoulder. "The rap you picked up in the Army was bullshit, and you know it. These guys, they understand how things get out of hand. You think you'd get kicked out of the Russian military for fighting? Hell, they'd have promoted you."

Cal glanced at his cheap Casio watch, nine p.m. "I got to be at work in an hour. I should start sobering up."

"Here I am trying to be a friend, and you're worried about getting to the cubicle farm so

you can waste your talents on schlubs that aren't worth half of you." Matt shook his head and ordered another round.

"Look, I know it ain't much, but it's honest work; you know I appreciate your friendship and all, but I just can't get wrapped up in this mess."

Their drinks arrived, and Matt pulled a hundred out of a stack of bills; those bills, it seemed to Cal, represented opportunity. He could almost see the disco lights reflecting off them.

They also stood for shady deals, waiting for drops, unanswered questions, always having to look over his shoulder. It was all the things he'd tracked as a cyber security specialist in the army, and yet so much worse. His loyalty flagged. America hadn't done shit for him, just used him up and cast him aside. Why should he maintain loyalty when he could just as easily reject them all and cash in?

The server took the bill.

"Keep the change," Matt said. He always did that. "Look, Cal, you think about it; I got a week before I head back. If you decide you want to make a change and make something out of yourself, you let me know, and I'll get you a plane ticket—first class. They got beds, roast duck, and wine up there."

Cal nodded and scratched the stubble on his chin as his friend got up and staggered toward the restroom. He fingered the loose change in his pocket while wondering if he'd have enough to grab a two-piece chicken meal and stash it in the office fridge before his shift started. Thoughts of blintzes and ocean fish smothered in exotic sauce wavered in front of his face. He cursed himself for not getting something at the bar while Matt was still buying. It was a tempting offer, but overall not worth it.

* * *

Work was at a low-rise office building on the edge of downtown, one of those anonymous concrete and glass blocks with no character or taste to it. They'd been putting them up all over the place since before Cal had ever set foot in Jackson, part of the city's expansion. The new, New South, that's how it was all over the country. As a younger man back in Owensboro, Kentucky, where Cal had grown up, he'd heard tell of folks working in new combination agriculture/pharmaceutical businesses they had going on; he didn't trust it. If they hadn't closed all the damn plants and laid off most of the folks down in the mines, they wouldn't need to be scraping fungus off corn or whatever they were doing.

Matt might have styled himself a good friend, but by the time Cal needed to get to his shift, his friend was neither in proper shape nor possessed the inclination to give Cal a ride. That meant the usual indignity of riding the bus into Jackson Station and waiting for a transfer.

Cal paced the platform, hands in pockets, old knapsack filled with his uniform and a portable DVD player slung over his shoulder, he checked the crappy watch on his wrist, 9:33 p.m.

Shit, he thought, he had to be at work by ten, and it took the bus a full half hour. More than five minutes late and they'd give him a point. *Points*, like he was a child, a kindergarten brat with sticky fingers. It was like that all over, everywhere he went, waiting around just to get scolded.

To save time he ducked back into the station and changed into his uniform, a nondescript gray shirt covered in patches and black jeans he had to buy himself; both looked as if he'd slept in them the night before. He'd collect the pepper spray and Maglite from his locker at the building. Security uniforms were usually meant to give the impression of authority to any intruder, while still being distinct from police wear, but to Cal, he just looked like a kid playing dress-up.

He wet a comb and ran it through his crew cut. He hadn't kept anything from his military days except the haircut—wouldn't be caught dead in an Army tee—but his hair wouldn't cooperate, just stood up and stuck out all over. Eventually he gave up and slammed all his supplies back into the bag. He rubbed the skin of his neck in the mirror. *I should have shaved, but really, no one would care.*

When he got back to the platform, his bus was pulling away. Cal swore and ran after it, his backpack swinging by his side. He caught up and pounded the glass on the doors.

"Hey, hey!"

The driver stopped short, his face a mask of annoyance. The doors swung open, and Cal hopped on board, pulling his pass out of his pocket.

"Thanks," he said, panting.

The driver grumbled, "Should have been waiting at the station. I can't stop for everyone running after me, you know. Dangerous too. Next time I won't—you be there or wait for the next bus."

Cal's blood spiked with rage, and he bit the insult off at the tip of his tongue. Not worth it, not today. In his old days, he'd have been ready to rumble, but he had to get to work. With a rictus grin, he found a seat near the middle next to an old man who smelled of grease and old engine oil. Cal checked the cheap Casio again. 9:45.

❄ ❄ ❄

Cal managed to slide in the access door at 10:30 just as a janitor was coming back from an early smoke break. She nodded sympathetically; he felt just a touch of solace in her glance. He shuffled down the stairs into the basement, taking them two at a time, to the tiny break room where his locker waited for him. Cal wasn't even sure why he was hurrying at this point; he was well and truly late, and no amount of running was going to prevent that. Maybe it was just force of habit; the smallest part of him that still wanted to please others.

He spun the combination on locker 4. The door never wanted to cooperate, so he had to jerk it open, cursing the whole way.

One of the day-shift guards, an older woman named Brenda, came in the room and effortlessly spun locker 2 open. "You better get up there," she said. "JD is in one hell of a mood; bad day to come in late."

Cal clipped his name badge onto his left breast pocket and grimaced something like a smile. "Thanks for the heads-up." He punched his card and turned to go.

He took the elevator up to the lobby. When he stepped out, he caught the profile of his boss, a thick-necked black man named JD Foster, speaking to a man in a crisp suit.

"Working late?" JD asked. He had a deep, rough, Baptist voice, the kind that's trained in choirs.

"You know it, JD," the man in the suit said. "Hell of a case; got this widow suing the John Deere company for her husband's death. One hell of a thing. She's in the right, but we ain't beating them—don't tell anyone I said that." The lawyer gave Cal's boss an expressive wink and a shake of his head. "World's going to hell, I swear."

"That's why I stay in church," JD said. "Going to go home and hug the wife, if my worthless employee ever decides to come in tonight."

Cal coughed, and stepped into sight. "Hello, Mr. Foster. Look, I'm really sorry."

"Oh, look who's here," JD barked, his voice filling the small lobby. "Singer, what you doing here? You decide to come into work tonight?"

"The bus was late."

"Late, huh?" JD's tone changed. The joviality slipped away. "Well, you know they got bus schedules now, don't you? You know they run late sometimes, don't you? You ever think of taking an earlier bus?"

The lawyer stepped backward, clearly uncomfortable at the chewing out. "I'll see you tomorrow, JD. You say hi to your wife for me."

JD held a hand up in farewell and waited for the front door to shut before he turned back to Cal. "I will never understand how a grown man can be late for work. That why they kicked you out of the Army … couldn't show up on time?"

Cal veins burned. "You know why. It was on my application."

"Yeah, I do, ain't you ever heard of humor? You know, you're lucky we gave you a job here." JD stood. "Been sitting at that desk for almost thirty minutes waiting on you, I don't think you appreciate us at all."

"I'm not asking for a favor. I work as hard as anyone else, and I deserve the same respect you do."

JD laughed. "I ain't the one got kicked out of the military for fighting, that's you. You can blame yourself for that. If you think you aren't getting what you deserve here, you know where the door is."

Unbidden, the image of Matt's stack of bills floated before Cal's inner eye; it conjured up images of nightclubs, hors d'oeuvres, satin sheets, and Audi sedans. Matt would be on a plane to Russia in a week, working for some oligarch, talking up ballet dancers, and eating dinner on white tablecloths.

The guy probably had a direct line to Vladimir Putin. Yeah, Putin might be a son of a bitch, a killer, and a crook, but who wasn't nowadays? At least Matt was getting real pay for real work, from people who understood what a man was worth. There wasn't any space left for decent men in Mississippi; hell, maybe not in any state in the U.S. and here Cal was with a head full of network architecture and cyber-warfare training, hands that knew how to take someone out quick as thought, getting chewed out by a guy in a shirt three sizes too small.

Cal reached up to his badge and tore it off. "Now that you mention it, I suppose I do, JD. I'm out of here."

"Now?" JD was shocked. "Who's working the night shift? There's a roast waiting for me at home."

Cal smiled, wider than he had in years; he was free. He was finally going to be someone.

"I'm keeping the Maglite," he said.

Outside the doors he took a deep breath of the humid air, which clung like a blanket. Cal pulled out his cellphone and dialed.

"Hey, Matt, you know who it is, sober up and come get me. Yeah, you said first class, right?"

Two

C al gazed at his boarding pass but try as he might he couldn't make out the words "First Class" anywhere on this sheet the kiosk had spat out for him. There was something about preferred boarding, and he was in Group C, which seemed right, but it still didn't quite make sense.

"Hey," he hollered across the concourse. "Hey, Matt."

Matt turned to face him, his carry-on rolling suitcase running into his legs. "Yeah, what's going on?"

Cal jogged a bit and caught up with him. "These boarding passes don't say first class. What gives?"

Matt looked at Cal's tickets, yanked them from his hand, and turned his head to the side in a big show of getting a good look. "This is just for the connecting flight, man. Don't sweat it—once we get to LaGuardia we'll be set."

Cal held out the other pass. "This one doesn't say it either."

"Look, if there's any confusion, we'll take care of it at when we get there. These airlines print all kinds of weird codes on these things. None of it means anything to guys like us."

Cal grunted, stashing the papers in his backpack along with his passport. The whole thing felt wrong ever since Matt came to his house at four in the morning to pick him up. Matt had been jittery, in far too much of a hurry given how they had plenty of time to get to their flight. He'd been gnashing his teeth, throwing Cal's luggage into the trunk without a thought as to what might be in there, slamming the lid, and cussing the whole time. If he had to guess, Cal would have chalked it up to amphetamine use, but he didn't want to assume. Besides, he thought, who doesn't need a pick-me-up now and again?

When he asked, Matt just grunted and muttered something about being up all night. And considering the stench of cigarettes wafting off his clothes and the redness of his eyes, Cal believed him without a doubt. What was worrisome wasn't so much the all-nighter as the unknown reason for it. Matt drove them the whole way to Jackson–Medgar Wiley Evers International Airport with his cellphone in one hand, furiously tapping out emails and text messages as he swerved between traffic. Matt wasn't the most careful driver—when behind the wheel he had both the technique and disposition Cal expected of a man who grew up learning to drive on the New Jersey Turnpike—but this was beyond the pale even for him.

And now, as they lined up at the security checkpoint, Matt was still muttering. He all but snatched his papers back from the person checking tickets. Then he spent the next several minutes carefully checking and rechecking his laptop bag and carry-on, taking things out, putting them back in, seemingly trying to organize them perfectly for the TSA agents. He snapped at an elderly woman ahead of him to hurry up, even as he tried to organize his laptop and multiple external hard drives.

Cal, for his part, decided to make up for his friend's rudeness and scatterbrained demeanor by being as calm about passing through the checkpoint as possible. He gave a fake smile as he handed his ticket and passport over, undid his belt and shoes ahead of time, and placed his sparse belongings in the right bins. This was already a tricky situation, given the surely quasi-legal status of whatever it was that awaited him in Moscow. The last thing he wanted to do was aggravate matters, single himself or his friend out as possible targets for the cops and rude, underpaid TSA security officers just looking for somebody to "make their day."

They waved Cal through the metal detectors. The alarm went off with a low honk, a sound surely intended to be less severe but nonetheless unnerving.

"Anything in your pockets?" the officer asked him.

His heart pounded a bit, but he found a rogue lighter in his pocket and passed it through. "Didn't realize I had that on me," Cal said with a sheepish grin. They motioned for him to go through again. No sound. He breathed a sigh of relief and set about repacking his bags and pockets.

Cal tied his right sneaker and stood up to go, duffel and backpack slung over his shoulders. He looked around for Matt, finally spotting him on a bench staring at the ground, shoes untied, hair further mussed.

Cal walked up to his friend. "What's wrong?" he asked. "Looks like you just stuck your finger in a light socket."

Matt looked up at him. "They're searching my bags."

"Oh shit, well, that really shouldn't mean anything, they do that all the time."

Matt shook his head with as much strength as he could muster. Whatever he was on, he was coming off it. "Get your head out of your ass. I can't have them finding anything in there."

"And what exactly could they find in there?"

Matt looked away, then back at Cal, it was as if he was making an appraisal, taking stock. "Nothing of course, nothing; why would I be worried?" he said with an unconvincing grimace of a smile. "Boy, am I tired, did I tell you I didn't sleep last night, I was so excited? I didn't sleep a wink, we're going to Russia, baby." The last sentence was so loud other passengers stared him down with disapproval.

The whole interaction shook Cal; for the first time it occurred to him that his friend was nothing more than a bag man for his mysterious employers, and that the story he'd been told, the lavish existence of good drinks and dance parties, was nothing but smoke and mirrors. Cal sized up the assorted police officers around the checkpoint. There was no running for it, no getting away from this. If Matt went down, he'd be going down too.

"Listen to me," Cal said to his friend, speaking quietly. "I'm not sure what all this is about, but you can't handle it when you're all messed up like this. You need to get your shit together before you get us both taken down and locked up, dammit, you hear me?"

Matt swallowed deep and nodded his head. "It's not even an issue; like I said, there's nothing in that bag. It's just pigs being pigs, you know. You know how that is—they're always looking for something."

Cal didn't appreciate the somewhat constant digs at his criminal record, but he made a motion in the affirmative and didn't broach the topic. The last thing he needed right now was to let his temper get away from him, not when he was on his way to a possible job interview with his very high friend. Cal had a feeling the Russians had a higher opinion of Matt than he did, and besides he needed Matt to vouch for him. Matt was just the kind of petty guy who would sabotage a friend over some meaningless disagreement. If this Russia thing didn't pan out, then Cal would be back on the road, looking for some other menial task well below his training and abilities.

The TSA agent waved over Matt, who turned white and stood, weak-kneed with ass perched. Cal watched him stumble, tennis shoes still untied. His friend talked with the agent, nodded his head, and repacked his bag. He turned around and flashed Cal a big smile.

"Laptop wasn't in the right bin," he said. Then, more quietly, "Fucking pigs, I tell you, who is this helping? No one, that's who. If I wanted to blow this place up—"

"That's great," Cal said, cutting him off. His concern hardened into genuine worry as Cal wondered what he'd gotten himself into.

※ ※ ※

They had to change planes at LaGuardia.

Matt stood at the gate, conversing with two airline employees. Their conversation wasn't audible to Cal, who had been instructed by his buddy to take a seat well away from the entrance with their stack of bags and just chill out while Matt "had a few words with these chumps" about something or other. A child began to squall nearby, his mother alternatively scolding and pacifying him with candy. Matt had taken Cal's boarding pass.

It was amazing to Cal how agitated this guy could look even from the view of his corpulent backside. He spoke with his hands, waving his arms, signifying what seemed like spaces in the air. His rumpled suit jacket twisted and contorted in what was either joy or impotent rage.

Cal had been through LaGuardia before, and while he thought its reputation as basically the worst airport in the country was a bit overstated, he had to admit it was a particularly difficult and confusing mess of a place to connect. They had to take a bus from one terminal to another, which set off another string of curses from Matt. He had slept on the connecting flight, but instead of improving his mood, the nap only served to make him more irritable upon being awoken. At least he was approaching something like lucidity.

The flight itself had been unpleasant, to say the least. Cal wasn't a short guy, and he'd had to fold his legs into the seat in front of him, constantly moving them into increasingly complex knots to keep blood-flow going and alleviate some of the pain. At one point both legs had gone completely numb. After sitting in coach for nearly three hours, Cal felt a quiet surge of gratitude for the fact that the upcoming transatlantic flight would be spent in glorious first class.

A third airline employee came up to speak with Matt. The argument seemed to escalate even further, as Matt's gestures became increasingly animated. He was bouncing up and down now, his heels leaving the dirty carpet as he shook his head, waving the boarding passes around and pointing at them. Cal suddenly put it together, and his heart sank. There had been some misunderstanding with the passes. They were for the wrong flight, or maybe the flight had been overbooked and they'd have to spend the night in LaGuardia, the part of Queens most forsaken by God.

The newest employee to arrive, who seemed to be some sort of a manager, took a step toward Matt, and Matt backed away, hands up, muttering something that sounded like an apology. He turned and picked his way through the clumps of tourists waiting to board, apparently trying to find the quickest route back toward Cal and their bags.

"All right," he began. "I've just spent I don't know how long trying to reason with this prick of an airline customer service rep, and I've got good news and bad news."

Cal sighed and balled his fists in the pockets of his hooded sweatshirt. "Let me have the bad news first."

"Well, see," Matt said and took a wadded up, dirty handkerchief from his inside pocket, then wiped his sweating forehead. "The good news is, the flight is on time. That's the good news."

Cal stared at him, empty. "I just said I wanted the bad news."

"Oh yes, you did. Well see, the bad news is, we are not in first class as I was told. It looks like they booked me for business class."

Cal felt his spirits rise just a bit. "That's not bad. It's not what you promised me, and I'll remember that, but I can take business class." He chuckled. "You had me worried. I thought the flight was delayed or all messed up."

"The flight's on time. Did I just say the flight is on time?"

"You did, and I'm happy about it."

"All right, well here's the bad news. You are not in business class."

"Then, where am I?"

Matt paused. "You're in economy plus."

It occurred to Cal that while Matt was much heavier, he was also a full head shorter and in far worse shape, which meant that it would be possible, with very little effort really, for Cal to beat his lying, treacherous ass right there in the waiting area, and probably put him down for several weeks before security would even get a chance to try and Taser or arrest him.

"Economy," Cal barked, struggling to control his voice. "You put me in economy."

"What did I just say? You're in economy plus."

"Yeah, big difference there."

"You'll get all kind of legroom, and they'll give you a free sandwich. You like roast beef, right?"

"I can't believe this." Cal's voice rose. "You show up sleep-deprived and all high on God knows what, you almost get us nabbed at security for whatever trash you're smuggling in your bag, and now I got to fly halfway across the world in economy."

"Hey, keep your voice down." Matt looked over both shoulders. "And it's economy plus."

"I don't care what it is. I want to know how you screwed up this badly."

"Don't look at me. I didn't book the tickets. It's all on my boss. He can be a real cheap bastard. You think I'm happy about having to fly business class? You ever tried to sleep on one of those beds?"

"You get a bed!"

"Look, I'll talk to the boss man. On the flight back we'll both be sitting pretty in the sky sipping champagne. The real stuff, none of this Korbel shit."

It was futile to argue, Cal realized. There was nothing for it. He'd have to make his peace with being packed into a stinking airliner like cattle. His legs already ached. The child nearby started wailing again with increased enthusiasm. Cal sighed and took his boarding pass back from Matt.

✿ ✿ ✿

"I want you to know that I'm not angry," Cal said. They sat in a tiny room somewhere in the bowels of Sheremetyevo International Airport. "But we need to talk about what happened back there."

"Not now," Matt groaned. "I need a drink."

The flight over had been, as Cal had expected, nothing short of a minor type of hell. Restful sleep had been entirely out of the question. He couldn't stretch his legs, and the neck pillow he'd hastily purchased a few days before was lumpy and stank of formaldehyde and foam rubber. The screaming child had been seated only a couple rows away, and since Cal owned earbuds but not full noise-cancelling headphones, the periodic howls woke him up every time. The roast beef was dry, on stale bread. But by then he was starving and wolfed it down like a good steak.

It wasn't the crappiness of the flight that was getting Cal down, however. That hadn't helped his mood, but he was willing to chalk it up to an error on the part of his future employer. Maybe the secretary hadn't realized the nature of Matt's request for another ticket.

No, it was the fact that they'd been taken into this back office so they could be interrogated by customs.

Their bags had been searched. Cal wasn't worried about his. He'd brought nothing but clothes, a few sports magazines, and an ancient laptop. They'd been nice enough about it, and the agent welcomed him to Russia with a smile.

But when it came time to search Matt's bags, they'd produced no less than six orange pill bottles and not enough prescription slips to account for all of them. Matt tried to play it off, said that he must have misplaced the paperwork and if they could just call his doctor it would all be taken care of. This didn't go over well, and the smiles turned to stone.

"Please come with us," a particularly grim officer had directed.

So that's how they found themselves here. Matt had attempted to launch into an explanation, but Cal wasn't interested. This was not how he'd planned on arriving in Russia. He'd been hoping for a limo ride through the streets of Moscow, where he'd be dropped off at a plush hotel and he could nap on first-rate sheets until he had to put on decent clothes and meet his new boss. Instead he was stuck here in a room that smelled of vinegar, lit by a single malfunctioning fluorescent tube.

The door opened, and in walked a thin, balding man in a cheap suit, a sheaf of papers in hand. His sharp features and wispy gray hair reminded Cal of a possum.

"Which of you is Matthew Hussy?" he asked with a thick accent but excellent pronunciation.

Matt stood and extended his hand. "Pleasure, I'm sure. What seems to be the issue."

The customs agent looked at the hand, then to Cal. "Calvin Singer?"

"Yes, sir," said Cal.

"You can have a seat."

Matt sat down, grumbling. Cal shot him a look, praying that his friend would finally develop the rudiments of charisma.

"Tell me about what we find in your bag, Mr. Hussy," the agent said.

"I don't know what you're talking about," Matt said. "There is nothing in that bag that I can't bring into this country. The whole thing is a mistake from the top to the bottom, and you're wasting our damn time. We have a meeting to get to."

The agent sighed and folded his hands. "If you insist on lying this takes much longer. Please, honesty, Mr. Hussy."

"I am being honest. Look, let's just take care of it now." Matt pulled out his wallet and the gigantic stack of American currency, and Cal's heart sank. "How much to make this all go away? I'm a businessman, you see. My time, our time, yours and mine, it's too valuable to waste on this. You've got smugglers two rooms over to bust. This can be really easy."

The agent stared at the money. His immovable rodent-like face creased slightly. "Bribery is very serious crime, Mr. Hussy."

"Are you kidding me? Do you know who I work for?"

"Excuse me," Cal said. He didn't know much, but he knew when he was in trouble, and he knew what tone worked at times like these. "If you don't mind me speaking, sir."

The agent nodded.

"My friend and I, we have had a terribly long flight. My friend, Mr. Hussy, Matt, he's a real sick fellow. All kinds of health problems with his heart, chronic pain, ADHD, the whole works." He adopted his sweetest Kentucky accent, the kind reserved for ornery grandmothers. "The Lord hasn't been kind to him. He needs his medication, but sometimes he forgets things. He usually takes this flight without me, but then he had to go out of his way to pick me up. Things got moved around, and that's how we find ourselves here."

The agent was silent for a moment, then gave the smallest grin. "Your friend here is much better spoken than you, Mr. Hussy. I wish we could let him do all the talking." He looked through some papers. "The medication does not concern us. Is mostly for bad heart, anyway. What I do want to know is why you have three hard drives, Mr. Hussy?"

Matt opened and closed his mouth. He fiddled with his suit jacket and rubbed his chin stubble. Finally, he turned to Cal and began to speak. "Well, see."

"Sir," Cal cut in. "We are businesspeople. There's a lot of documents we must carry. Real estate you see, very advanced blueprints and renderings of buildings. My associate here, he's building up all kinds of new places all over the state of Mississippi. And of course, we got investors, developers, all kinds of folks out here in your beautiful country just aching to come down and buy up space in our towns and cities. We can't send all that stuff via email, FTP isn't secure enough, and we've been having just the worst bandwidth issues. So, we thought, let's just bring it on down here in person and show it off."

There was more silence. The agent shuffled through the papers in front of him. "What is your line of work, Mr. Singer?"

"Security," Cal said without thinking, then cursed himself.

"You are bodyguard?"

He turned and looked at Matt. "Yes, I'm afraid so."

"You talk about computer a lot for bodyguard."

Cal gave a bitter smile. "You need to know all kinds of things to work security nowadays."

The agent gave a small noise of assent. "You said to call your boss," he said to Matt. "What is your boss's name?"

"Sokolov," Matt said, and he began running his hands furiously through the business cards in his wallet. "I got his number right here, hang on." He handed one to the agent.

"Be right back." The agent left the room. The door locked behind him.

Matt let out a low whistle. "I think we dodged it. Good job, man."

"Why do you have three hard drives, Matt?" Cal asked quietly.

"Like you said," Matt smiled. "Bandwidth issues."

***

They stood shoulder to shoulder at the terminal, waiting for a car to come and pick them up. Cal put the fantasies of hotel beds out of his mind. Matt had informed him that with all the time wasted, they'd be going straight to the boss's house, with no opportunity to wash up or change. Apparently, punctuality was valued in these parts, and Matt's indiscretions had violated that somewhat.

All things considered, the agent wasn't gone very long once he took the card and made his phone calls. He'd come back, apparently satisfied that things were as above board as could be expected. There was an implication, maybe in his handshake or the tone of his voice, that it would be best for all involved if they never met again, that if Matt found himself in a room like this again the outcome would be very different.

"So, who's coming to pick us up?" Cal asked. "Is it a guy in a 1976 Alfa Romeo? Or are we going to have to take one of these shitty cabs?"

"Why so down, Buster Brown?" Matt said. He gave a brief whistle.

"I'm just trying to figure out how y'all plan on fucking up this time."

Matt's mood had improved considerably since landing and going through the ordeal with customs, far too much to be normal. It was almost as if they'd passed a test of some sort. Cal idly wondered if the whole thing had been a bit of theater, a pre-interview for whatever it was that he was expected to do over here.

"Are you a bag man?" he asked Matt.

"Do I look like a bag man?" Matt snapped. "I mean, does a bag man wear a Rolex?"

"Your Rolex is fake. I don't know nothing about watches, and I can tell your Rolex is fake, if you make so much money, why can you not at least invest in a real time piece."

"What is your deal, man? I'm hooking you up here. I'm setting you up with the good times, and you're put off because of a couple snags."

"I just flew economy and almost got arrested by customs."

"Economy plus. And by the way, you did great back there." Matt slapped Cal on the back. "Just perfect. Sokolov is going to love you, I can already tell."

A late-model Mercedes-Benz glided up to the curb in front of them. A big hairy guy in an old sweater got out of the driver's seat and walked around the front.

"Grigori!" Matt called out. He reached out and shook the man's hand. "How you been, you son of a bitch?"

Grigori shrugged. "Still healing from gallbladder. We talk in car. Boss is mad."

Matt laughed nervously. "What's new, right? Something always climbing up the old dog's asshole."

The driver chuckled. "Yes, always. Who is friend?"

"This," Matt said, presenting his friend with a flourish, "Is my man Cal."

"Cal." Grigori reached out to shake. His massive paw all but crushed Cal's hand, and Cal leaned all his strength in return, let him know he meant business. The sleeve of Grigori's sweater pulled up a bit, and Cal spied a tattoo.

"Good to meet you, Cal. Come, put bag in trunk, we are late."

The trunk slid open on pristine pneumatics without a sound. Matt and Cal stashed their bags in the cavernous expanse, and they each took a seat in the back.

"See," Matt said, buckling up. "And you thought I was full of shit."

Cal grunted assent and leaned back against the headrest, turning his head to look out the window as they pulled away. At that point, there was little anyone could do to convince him this wasn't a terrible mistake, and while the seats were leather and the windows were tinted, it didn't do much to assuage how lost and empty he felt.

But he had to admit, as they pulled onto the highway and the environs around Moscow came into view, that there was something beautiful about being here. Cal had never been in Russia before and had been unsure if the capital would be a hypermodern metropolis or a total dump. The reality seemed to be a bit of both. Many of the cars were fifty years old or at least looked like it—ugly, boxy little deals. Ugly gray towers, housing obviously built during the Soviet era, stood alongside half-completed skyscrapers, massive cranes lazily keeping watch.

It had been a long day, or more like two days. Cal tried to arrange his thoughts, prepare something for the first meeting with his new boss. Yet there was no struggling against fatigue. He decided to close his eyes, just for a moment. Matt would wake him if he fell asleep.

***

Matt, as it turned out, did not wake him up until they were almost to the house.

"Hey man," he said, shaking Cal. "We're here. Come on, get your shit together."

Cal woke with a start, banging his head against the window. Disoriented, he looked around as the Mercedes slowly wove its way toward their destination. This was no longer the charming mix of old and new. Every building here, wherever they were, was dilapidated, a product of old and neglected construction. None of the signs were in English, and the road was far bumpier, with lots of potholes. Random children ran back and forth in vacant lots, harassing the stooped grandmothers who walked by, laden with shopping bags.

The driver pulled the car onto a side road, and they drove even further from what civilization there was into a more wooded area.

"Grigori," Cal said. "Are we still in Moscow?"

"Ah, no," he said. "We are in Breznygrad."

Cal turned to Matt.

"It's in the Moscow oblast," Matt said with a valiant attempt at levity. "And did I say we were going to Moscow? No, I said Russia. You're in Russia. Enjoy yourself. We're here."

Grigori pulled up to a gated driveway and spoke into the intercom in quick brutal Russian. He turned around to them and shook his head. "Boss is in terrible mood."

"Yeah," Cal said. "I'm used to that."

They drove up toward the house, an aging but sizable mansion built in a vaguely neoclassical style. The landscaping left something to be desired in both taste and quality, with massive overgrown bushes spilling all over spotty lawns. Yet from the outside it still looked like a nicer home than any Cal had been in. He found that thought to be rather depressing.

The Mercedes came to a stop, and Grigori cut the engine.

"Any advice?" Cal asked.

"Don't look ready for fight," Grigori said.

Cal nodded. Sure, he'd just rewrite his whole personality.

They got out of the car, and the front door opened. At least half a dozen people spilled out, men of various sizes with an odd assortment of clothes: some combination of athletic wear and country club fashion seemed to be the default. The one guy in a suit (but no tie) was older and heavier than any of them, like a retired wrestler. His forehead deeply furrowed, his face like well-worn saddle leather bearing a permanent frown. Cal thought, this guy couldn't smile of his life depended on it. He took his time walking over to them.

"Mr. Sokolov," Matt said. "How the hell are you?"

Sokolov considered him for a moment. "You are late." His voice was impossibly deep, and the most heavily accented Cal had yet heard. "Why are you late?"

"Things didn't go too well at the airport," Matt said, an edge of fear in his voice.

"I heard. I heard that you were detained at customs and had to make phone call. What was it this time, Matty? Was it pills?"

"Afraid so," Matt confessed but intentionally remained silent about the hard drives.

Sokolov took out a cigarette and lit it. "Why do you bring pills on business trip Matty? We have pills here. You could ask any of us; pills for your back, pills for your head, what is wrong with you?"

"I'm sorry sir."

Sokolov's men formed a semicircle behind him. They filled the air with a sense of casual violence. "Are you idiot Matty? Are you just dumb ass? You have important job, and you bring drugs. You are idiot."

"You got me," Matt said, trying to smile. "I'm an idiot."

"Who is your friend?"

Cal held out his hand. "My name is Calvin Singer, sir. Very pleased to meet you, Mr. Sokolov."

Sokolov gave him a couple weak shakes. "Are you also dumb ass?"

"No, sir, I'm a smart ass."

Sokolov finally gave a laugh, a single, dangerous bark. "Funny guy." He turned back to Matt. "This is serious, Matty. This is not good for you. How many times you get stuck at customs? Do I take you out to woods? Do I cut you open and let the bears eat you and your friend? Tell me, Matty."

Just then, the front door flew open and a dark-haired young woman stuck her head out, screaming in Russian. Sokolov turned and began yelling back, and she stepped outside with bare feet, meeting his volume. She dressed like an art student, all scarves and flowing skirts, and Cal could not help but notice she was extraordinarily attractive.

Finally, with a single curse, the woman turned and went back inside.

Sokolov turned back and rubbed his forehead with the hand holding the cigarette. "Sorry, my youngest daughter, Polina Popov, she is visiting. Takes after her mother, drives me crazy." He sighed. "I am being too harsh, Matty, I am embarrassing you in front of this friend you bring to work for us." Sokolov put an arm around

Matt and the other around Cal. "So next time you fuck up, I feed you to the bear, is that all right with you?"

"Yes," Matt squeaked. "I'll feed myself to the bears if I fuck up again, Mr. Sokolov. Don't worry about that."

"That's good, come, let's get drunk."

As he was marched to the house by his new employer, fresh off economy plus, being detained by customs, and threatened with disembowelment, Cal knew that he should feel like a wreck and afraid for his well-being. But then he thought of Polina, and things didn't seem so bad anymore.

Three

The inside of Sokolov's mansion matched the outside: expansive and well built, but depressingly shabby. The sitting room he guided Matt and Cal into was littered with old-fashioned ornate furniture, all fake-gilded wood and brocade. Soviet-era ephemera filled glass cabinets and battered tables, and an old AK-47, polished to a mirror shine, hung on the wall. A bottle of Beluga Gold vodka, mostly full, sat on the coffee table along with a few shot glasses.

By this point, Cal had realized it would be best to temper his expectations. Nothing about this had turned out the way he envisioned, and it became clear, as he took a seat next to Matt on a particularly dumpy couch, that he had been sold a false bill of goods. That said, he resolved to make the most of it. There was still clearly an opportunity at hand here, or else Sokolov would have presumably made good on his threats of feeding them to bears, or some other less theatrical, more efficient method of disposal. Cal looked at the rifle and idly wondered if it was loaded.

Sokolov followed his gaze and smiled, as if he read Cal's mind. "It is ceremonial rifle, from my good old days in the KGB. You must excuse me; I am an old man and very prone to nostalgia."

Cal gave a half-smile. He, too, at times thought wistfully of his time in the service of his country. "Is all of this KGB stuff?" he asked.

Sokolov nodded his head to the affirmative. He walked to one of the cabinets and tapped on the glass, waving Cal over. Cal looked through the window and saw an assortment of medals. "This one I got for service to country. Stopped large West German spying operation, organized by CIA. And this one was for operation during Afghanistan war. We fought against Taliban dogs." He smiled, clearly relishing the opportunity to brag. "Your country funded them."

"With all your background in the military, how did you ever get interested in an American enterprise? Were you always interested in America's businesspeople and its economy?" Cal asked. He sensed it was a risky question.

"Indeed. I have always had good understanding of American mind. You are far prouder of businesspeople than the Russians have been. Both great strengths, but also terrible weakness." He pointed at a bust of Vladimir Lenin. "That one and rifle, I bought myself. Very valuable. I respect people's struggle. Fighting is very hard work, but nowadays, they do not fight for anything, it is all business. Blessing and curse, I suppose. So now I do industry, lumber, shipping, that sort of thing. Different kind of service."

The outside door slammed, and Grigori walked in with their luggage. He left most of it in the hall except for Matt's computer bag, which he threw to its owner. Matt held onto it, nonplussed.

Sokolov stared at him with increasing impatience. "Well?"

"Oh," Matt said. "You want to do this now?"

"Why else are you here?"

Matt opened the bag and took out his laptop, along with one of the drives, placing both on the table before plugging them in. He typed for a few moments, then swiveled the computer around to show Sokolov. Cal tried to get a good look—he saw a file called DONORS.zip—but Matt was too fast.

Sokolov looked at the screen for a few minutes that felt like hours. Finally, he nodded, closing the machine. "Well, I suppose you are not all useless." He chuckled, and Cal realized that the Russian oligarch was not in the habit of giving compliments. "And the rest is there too?"

"I can show you," Matt said, a bit too loudly. "There's more on the other drives."

"Why do you have more drives?"

"Ah. Technical difficulties?"

Sokolov frowned. "Dangerous to be carrying around like that. Put it all on one next time."

"Sure thing."

At last Sokolov relaxed. He picked up the bottle of vodka and poured, motioning to the Americans. "Come, drink, this stuff is not bad." He lifted his own glass. "To new business associates!" He appended something in Russian before draining the shot.

37

Cal brought the glass to his lips and drank. The liquor was cool, and smoother than he expected. Sokolov refilled their glasses, toasted, and drank again, before filling them a third time. He sat back in his chair, folding his hands and giving Cal a long, appraising look.

"So, your name is Calvin Singer, yes?" he asked.

"Yes, sir. I usually go by Cal."

"You go by Cal? You Americans and your nicknames." Sokolov shook his head. "Always so informal. In Russia, we often think of people with both names. So, Calvin Singer, what is it that you can do?"

"Well, I'm trained as a cybersecurity specialist. Done a lot of systems administration work, as well as counterintelligence."

Sokolov raised a brow. "You are good with computers, then? Maybe you can help Matty here to make better files." He filled their glasses yet again. "Where you go to university?"

Cal swallowed. "I was trained in the United States Army, sir."

"Oh, so you're a military man. And you do what, now?"

"I'm a security guard. So, I'm not exactly using my full potential."

"I see, why do you leave military?"

"If you don't mind, I'd rather not say."

Sokolov frowned. "What do you mean, you rather not say? This is important thing to know."

"I'm afraid it's rather embarrassing, sir." Cal turned up the Kentucky charm. "And I must say, it ain't the kind of story to just go on about here. You understand how a man can be rather ..."

He trailed off as the boss's daughter wandered back into the room. Polina had a surprising grace about her, all dark flowing hair and legs. Here, in this dumpy yet also exotic sitting room she seemed to exude a palpable charisma, as if they should all consider themselves blessed by her appearance.

Then she opened her mouth and let out a string of harsh Russian towards her father, which somehow both broke the spell and enhanced her beauty in Cal's eyes. He knew it was just the typical fetishization of accents, but he still found the effect pleasant, overall.

Sokolov's gaze darkened as he muttered a response to her. The boss didn't seem afraid of his daughter exactly, but he did show a deference that Cal recognized. This was a man who, for all his gruff posturing, doted on his bratty daughter, and now found himself torn between the needs of his business and the demands of his daughter.

At last he sighed and switched back to English. "Calvin Singer, this is my daughter, Polina Popov, she insists upon using her mother's name."

Cal jumped to his feet and extended a hand, Polina laid hers in it. "What do you do for my Papa, Calvin Singer?" she asked. Her English was heavily accented and dusky.

"Oh well, I'm afraid I don't have the honor of working for him yet." He laughed nervously. "I'm a cybersecurity expert."

"I am sure you will be soon, and you will be paid very well for your service," she said, glaring at Sokolov. "Papa is much more generous with business than family." Then she asked her father, "Will we be leaving soon?"

Sokolov groaned and looked at Cal with a slightly humorous expression. He spoke briefly in Russian, and Polina left the room in a minor huff, apparently satisfied.

"You must forgive her," Sokolov said. "My daughter, she is very spirited. High-strung university girl. I am sure you have her type in America."

"Boy, do we," Matt said with a dirty laugh. Cal kicked his dress shoes.

"Yes, she only come to visit twice a year. She is very busy with her studies, you see. So, since we do not see her often, Polina demands we go out for dinner. And since we have such fine guest, I think we all go out and continue conversation?"

"You sure that's ideal, Mr. Sokolov?" Matt asked.

Cal kicked him again. "Mr. Sokolov, I think that would be an excellent idea."

The boss smiled and stood. He motioned them toward the door, calling for Grigori. It occurred to Cal that his friend Matt could be kind of an idiot, and he prayed that he would be too busy stuffing his face with a free meal to make them look any worse than they already did.

❖ ❖ ❖

Grigori, Polina, and Sokolov took one car, leaving Matt and Cal with a different, far more reticent driver. Cal had been raven-ously hungry in the car, but upon entering and being greeted with potent new odors, his interest in food dropped entirely.

When the waiter came to take their order, Sokolov spoke for the whole table. At first Cal thought it had something to do with the menus being written entirely in Cyrillic, but he realized it was just as much about power: Sokolov held all the authority here. No one had called ahead for a reservation, and yet they were still seated at an expansive table well away from prying eyes or lumbering servers, a bottle of wine appearing without the slightest word or sign being uttered.

Cal and Matt shared the table with the boss, his daughter, and Grigori. Their driver waited outside, apparently not worthy to take part in the conversations to be had. There also seemed to be a good chance he was there to serve as a lookout. Sokolov conversed briskly with Grigori, who seemed to be not simply a driver but a kind of second-tier body man for his employer. They shared laughs and sober reflections alike, all of it in Russian and none of it seeming to have anything to do with what Cal was there to do, which was to get employed.

The restaurant itself was, to Cal, bizarre. It kept with the antiquated environs of Breznygrad, but this time it felt more like an approximation of a formal dining room circa 1923. It was a real white tablecloth joint with tattered carpets, serving massive portions of bland Russian food. The patrons seemed far more well-off than the citizens of the surrounding town Cal had observed on the car ride over. It all came together to give Cal a sense of quiet desperation, as if prosperity was returning to this impoverished place but hadn't quite made it there yet.

Cal scooted the *pelmeni* around his plate, forlorn. There was nothing overtly wrong with the moderately spiced, slightly undercooked little dumplings, but the stuffy white tablecloth atmosphere and his host's chattering, unintelligible conversation put him off what appetite he should have had. He'd already stuffed down a serving of cold borscht studded with chopped prawns and a few bits of shockingly gritty beluga roe, and the pickle-like sour cream smell permeated everything until he had trouble breathing.

At last Sokolov wiped his mouth and, pouring himself more wine, broke back into English, addressing Cal directly. "Now, Mr. Singer. Perhaps we continue where we left off?"

"You said no business," Polina cut in. Cal took notice of her careful use of English and took the subtle hint, only slightly annoyed that she was attempting to derail this further. She had kept an eye on him all through the meal up to this point. He'd be angry at her if she wasn't so attractive.

"I'm terribly sorry to intrude like this, Ms. Popov," Cal said. "It's just, I've flown a very long way, and your father and I have much to discuss."

"So, have I," she said. "I come from Moscow to see Papa. Very rare for me, maybe come twice a year. Much to say."

"I understand, Ms. Popov. But that's just how it is."

She grunted. Polina had barely touched anything throughout the meal, which explained her slight, waiflike figure. "You do not understand. Papa is always busy with one thing or another. Ship this here, talk to guy there. Get gun, shoot this man or another, push him off hotel balcony."

"Polina," Sokolov said, with enough brute force to shut her down. Polina went silent and stared off, her mouth fixed in a scowl. "Now then. What is it you have been doing, Calvin?"

"I've been doing all kinds of things, Mr. Sokolov. I'm a real jack of all trades, I can wear many hats." Seeing that the idioms didn't land on his future employer's face, Cal corrected himself. "I mean to say, I know how to do lots of stuff. Like I said, I'm mostly trained for cybersecurity. And obviously I know my way around a rifle, and I'm handy in a fight."

"Ah. You said you left military. Why?"

Grigori lent over. "Be honest. Boss more open-minded than he seems." His voice had a tone of confidentiality, even though everyone could hear him.

"Yeah, Cal, just spit it out," Matt said. He was already drunk.

Cal took a deep breath. Asking for a confession like this, to just be blurted out, seemed rude at best and career-killing at worst. He had learned quickly that whenever a potential employer asked to hear the full story of his exit from the armed services, a bit of massaging was necessary. If Cal told them what had happened at face value, just said that he'd punched a well-connected superior officer with a very promising career and broke the young man's good arm, whoever was hiring would just shut down. They wouldn't be interested anymore; would say he was overqualified or that they were looking for someone less spirited.

In time he'd learned to lie, to give as little information as possible. He'd say he was ejected on a technicality, related to a good-natured wrestling match between friends that had gotten out of hand, and subtly imply that the system had been against him. This earned him the barest bit of sympathy. He would still be seen as a joke, a dangerous guy to be used and disposed of as soon as possible. And besides, how many decent Americans wanted to believe there was corruption in the military? Especially when that testimony was coming from the mouth of an admitted failure, a man who couldn't cut the mustard and had been unceremoniously booted on his ass. There was no escaping the fact that he'd been kicked out for assault. Any background check would show that as the truth.

But here, in a shitty restaurant in some uninteresting, small, blighted suburb in the "Moscow oblast," the truth didn't seem so horrifying. These were gangsters, no doubting that. The tattoos, man the tattoos, they all had them, one in particular a guy had his shirt un buttoned to his waste, Cal could see a dagger piercing the man's chest skin, first in then out again, from left to right, like a sewing needle. He'd seen some of these in the past and knew immediately that this one meant that this guy had been in prison. This man had killed a fellow prisoner and now that he was out, he was open for business, hire for a kill. He even had 2 blood droplets falling from the dagger tip, which meant he had taken two lives so far. There was much KGB memorabilia, the open threat of mauling by bear, it was all too clear that he was entering business with the Russian mob. Would they care about what happened? Would Cal be violating some unspoken code of honor, outed as a traitor, or would they see him as an asset, sympathetic to the Russian cause on account of his rejection from the American one?

Fuck it, Cal thought. He resolved to tell the truth in more detail than he had in years.

"I went into the Army as soon as I could, and I got as good a training as I could," he said. "Got the best grade I'd ever gotten in my whole life, so they put me on this base out in Maryland, and they had me do all this networking stuff, mostly making sure our systems are working right and ain't going to be hacked."

"And were you good at it?" Sokolov asked.

Here Cal felt the need to embellish. "I was one of the best they had. But then again, I didn't get into the military to stare at a screen all day. I've always liked fighting, getting into it with people who don't know how to act. Respect is really important where I'm from, and I've never gotten much of it to speak of, so, since I didn't get to go to Iraq or Afghanistan and kick some jihadi ass, I started to get pretty wound-up."

Sokolov nodded. "Middle East was always uncivilized. Would have been good for you to go there."

"That's what I thought, but they never saw fit to deploy me. So, I started getting into it with my comrades. You got a whole bunch of men just raring to go, and you stick them in computer rooms all day; something is bound to give."

Grigori chuckled. "*Da*. We would box for fun back in my Army days."

Cal waved toward him, grateful for the backup. "Right, so, I get a couple reprimands for fighting, nothing major, but one night, out at the bar off base, some fresh-faced brat right out of officer's training decides he doesn't like how loud me and my buddies are getting. One of them had made a crack about my manliness, and I wouldn't stand for that. But this goody two-shoes starts telling us to settle down, and we do, but my buddy won't stop. So, I deck my friend to shut him up."

Everyone at the table laughed. Even Polina gave a small smile and began to listen more closely.

"The officer, he ain't having this, he tries to break us up, and I'm drunk and not sure what's going on. All I know is, somebody laid hands on me, so I'm inclined to lay them back. What else am I going to do? Turns out, he can't fight for shit, and I beat him good. But he's an officer, and his daddy was high up in the ranks. If he'd been an enlisted man, they might have busted me down to private. This kid was a lieutenant; that meant I was looking at a court-martial for assaulting a superior officer, which meant jail time. After all that, they weren't too keen to take me back. I went into civilian life, worked at the places that would take me. Then I meet Matty here, and he tells me what a fine fellow you are, and I say, well, I might as well come meet this great man you've been telling me about."

It all spilled out of Cal at once, and the extended confession left him winded. He drained his wineglass and folded his napkin. Sokolov considered him for a moment, stroking his chin, seemingly lost in thought. The large, rough faces of his hosts were impossible for Cal to read. Everyone he'd met so far had been dour and ready for violence, even in moments of levity. He turned to Matt, who looked at his boss, unwilling to break eyeline. Servers came by and cleared the plates, silver, and glasses.

"Sir?" Cal began.

Sokolov held up one hand, indicating his desire for silence. He muttered in Russian to Grigori, who responded in kind. Their facial expressions had changed during the earlier conversation, going from bored to amused and finally down to contemplative. Real fear returned to Cal, and it occurred to him that given how he had been brought to the boss's home and dined at his table, a sufficiently transgressive story might put his life in danger. Matt

46

didn't seem to be on the best of terms with his boss, especially considering the snafu with customs and his general air of sloppiness. It would be too easy to dump the two Americans in some remote forest and take all their ID. No one would miss them, and Russia was a big place. Their bodies would never be found, and that would be the end of Calvin Singer's short, inglorious tale.

Polina cleared her throat. "Most of you Americans are very weak," she began. Her attitude toward Cal had changed. Now she was far softer and more open. "You are victim of your system; it turns out weak, rich boys with soft hands."

The servers returned, bearing glasses of tea and slices of cake. Cal looked at his plate. His appetite had, if anything worsened, and while it seemed like an excellent piece of cake and by far the most attractive thing that had yet been put in front of him, it might as well have been rat poison for its appeal to him. He took the smallest bite he could, it was like ash.

At last Sokolov took his fork and shoved half of his cake into his mouth. He chewed, ruminating, before finally swallowing. "I hope you do not beat Grigori here," he said, chuckling. "Unsure you would live through the experience."

A small wave of relief filled Cal with warmth from the feet up. Finally, there was some bit of humanity present in this horrible place.

"So long as you do not cause trouble, I do not care what you have done," Sokolov continued. "You should not fight with superior, but if your superior cannot take you down then he was not worthy to be superior. Too many weak bureaucrats at upper levels of government."

"I would agree, sir," Cal said.

"Where are you from?"

"Kentucky, sir. Northern part of the state. Very proud of the South, if I do say."

Polina's eyes lit up, but she didn't say anything.

Sokolov grinned. "We have KFC, you know."

This singular point of reference endlessly repeated almost everywhere Cal went, it irritated him whenever it was brought up, but he ignored it. To him, Kentucky is more known for the Kentucky Derby or some of its tasty bourbon, why did it always have to be fried chicken? "Yes indeed. It's real lovely down there. I live in Mississippi right now, and I hope to die in a place that beautiful."

Polina leaned back in her chair smiling. Her father scowled and leaned forward in his.

"This what I need from you," he said. "Our computer guys, they are shit. The world is changing, and these old-fashioned bastards have no desire to change with it. They run businesses to take money from rich Western fools, and I do not have problem with that, but it does me no good."

"If you don't mind me asking, sir, what is it you do?"

Sokolov grinned. "Difficult question. We have lumber business, does very well. We ship all kinds of product all over country. But we also serve very important role in modern Russia. KGB is no more, and we do not have big national infrastructure like there used to be. It is all private industry now. That means us who used to be KGB, some of us become FSB. And some of us, we serve country in different ways."

Cal felt his heart rate increase. He leaned forward, ducking his head and with a wry grin, softly whispered, "So, you are spies is that right?"

Grigori shot him a look. "Spies do not say they are spies."

Sokolov waved his arm, indicating a vast space. "We keep peace around here. We keep an eye on things, make sure local government is not overstretched. We do so well, people in power ask us to do more. So now, we are helping with Russian interest in America. All capitalist industry of course, but all of it in service of the country."

"What do you need me for, then?"

"Information is now currency of the realm. Data is worth more than any lumber. If we do have American interest, then we will need better computer guy. We cannot have amateur risking things." Here, Sokolov gave the smallest glance towards Matt. "Instead, we need someone who can do good work, unafraid to get dirty, and willing to do what is needed. Are you that guy?"

Cal considered the implications. These weren't just gangsters. For all his talk of private industry, there was no way around the fact that Sokolov's mysterious benefactors and his talk of "data" sounded just as much like espionage as it did moving a bit of contraband. The risks were extreme, far worse than what he expected. Not that he hadn't expected there to be some amount of risk, but more like the risk involved with talking his way out of a possession charge than being tried for treason.

And besides, he was an American. What would it mean if he enabled these people who were clearly going against his country, taking or sharing information that rightfully should remain stateside? After this, he would no longer simply be an outcast but a full-on pariah, a de facto enemy of the state. Yes, he needed work, and every man has a price. But at what cost?

"You're asking me for a lot," Cal said.

"Yes, I know," Sokolov said. "And I wish I could pay better. You would have to stay here of course, I need my men close to me, at least at first. You must train here under my supervision; you need to know what your purpose is. It can only happen here with me at first. And I could only give you about twenty-five thousand a month."

Cal's heart sank. "Twenty-five thousand rubles isn't much."

Sokolov burst laughing. "I am saying twenty-five thousand US dollars; more or less, depending on your performance. Always chance for Christmas bonus."

Every man has his price and Sokolov had just named Cal's. All his concerns fled, and he laughed with shock and relief. "Mr. Sokolov, I'd be honored to join your organization."

"Good! Just don't fuck it up."

Everyone laughed with a combination of relief and genuine joy, even Polina. Sokolov called for vodka, and Matt clapped his buddy on the shoulder a bit too hard.

There would be further arrangements to make, of course. Sokolov made a vague mention of needing to get him a visa and having him be employed, at a much lower rate, for his official business. But that didn't really matter in the moment. What mattered was that progress had been made.

"We should celebrate," Matt said. "There's some bars not too far away, we should go and have some fun."

Polina spoke up. "My friends and I are going out tonight, you would be welcome to join—both of you." She said both, but looked only at Cal.

"Now Polina, you should not be imposing on our guests," Sokolov said. "They are tired. Let them have a nightcap. Besides, we barely see each other."

"I will see you tomorrow," she said. The edge came back into her voice. "I would be bad host did I not show new friend around." Polina gave a smile that Cal thought was a bit too flirty for a dinner with one's father.

Sokolov groaned. "I spoil you, child. You, Cal, treat my daughter well, da?"

Cal nodded. He would treat everyone well. He had been given an opportunity, and he would not squander it, not now that there was a second chance before him. He smiled, avoiding Polina's gaze. Maybe there was more than a second chance.

✿ ✿ ✿

The club Polina brought them to was, like everything else in the area, far older than what had been sold to Cal. A single disco ball hung from the ceiling, slightly cracked and askew, and the only music was loud nineties American pop and Russian-language disco. Nonetheless, the place was packed, and they had no problem getting in. Clearly, being the daughter of Sokolov had significant advantages.

The disco was a few towns over, not anywhere near Moscow proper but at least slightly less depressing than Breznygrad. The

51

silent driver had grunted with irritation as Polina briskly told him where they were going, clearly not looking forward to a lengthy drive after a long evening of waiting for his boss to eat dinner while he was relegated to a burger. Cal wanted to say something, remind him that Polina was his boss's daughter, and that he himself was about to make decent money, not drive a car around. But he held his tongue and settled next to her in the back seat.

They got a table in the corner. A bottle of tequila was brought over, much to Cal's surprise. Somehow, he expected that they wouldn't have anything from North America out in this part of the world, but then he chided himself. Imports were more than possible and always had been, even in the Soviet era, when smuggling and a web of alliances had allowed all sorts of decadent Western items into the Easter Bloc, albeit at often ridiculous prices.

Polina's two friends were as attractive as she was. Thin, statuesque young women with various hair colors, all in tight dresses. Polina's attire was more causal, which made her stick out but also gave her an almost unnatural grace.

Both of her friemds suffered through Matt's clumsy advances. He complimented their bodies and clothes with his typical New Jersey lack of style, offering brusque comments that offended what little decorum Cal had. Thankfully, they spoke very little English, which allowed Matt to convince them to dance, leaving Polina and Cal alone at the table.

Sighing, she picked up the tequila bottle. "To new friends," she said over the music, drinking right from the bottle.

Cal nodded. "*Nostrovia*," he yelled back, taking a swig.

She laughed and said something he couldn't hear.

"What?"

She leaned over to speak into his ear. "That's not the correct way to say it, it is *Na Zdorovie*. You Americans are so funny," she said. "Do you want to go outside?"

He nodded, and they went outside on the dinky back patio. She offered him a cigarette, and though he hadn't smoked in years, he accepted. It was cold, and Cal was having trouble staying upright, what with the endless flight and all the booze.

"You are from the South? I love *Gone with the Wind*. Was favorite movie."

"I am," he said. "It's a beautiful place."

She smiled and put a hand on his chest. "I have always wanted to go there. Since I was a child."

"Maybe one day I'll take you there."

"I would like that. I have always wanted a large plantation house, lots of land, and horses. Is it anything like that?"

There wasn't a damn thing similar between the coal-mining town of Owensboro and the sweeping plantation vistas of Georgia, but Cal decided to run with it. It was nice, in any case, not to have someone reference Kentucky Fried Chicken, first off.

"There are places like that. I live in a city named Madison, just outside the capital city of Jackson in the state of Mississippi."

"You should move out to country. Have farm. Get a wife."

"I'm a bit away from that. I mean, I just got myself a job."

She reached up and kissed him on the cheek. "It may be sooner than you think."

Four

C al stared at the security logs on the battered laptop in front of him and shook his head. He hated this part of the job; it wasn't the language barrier that frustrated him this time. He'd gotten used to switching back and forth on these old systems between Russian and English, and besides, UNIX shell scripts were a universal language.

No, what he hated was that he was looking at undeniable evidence that the laptop had been used to funnel secrets to one of Sokolov's Ukrainian rivals.

The machine's owner cowered in the corner, a thin, middle-aged man with a face stricken with terror. Grigori held him in the chair by his collar while the silent driver (whose name Cal still hadn't managed to learn even after a full year in Sokolov's employ) looked on. The owner was nobody, some functionary who moved money around for the boss. Something had gone missing, which is why he had come over in a separate car. All Cal had to do was look and see what the owner had been up to. But he knew what came next.

Cal swallowed and turned to Grigori. "Well."

Grigori nodded. "Yes?"

"Looks like our boy here's been sending a few too many messages to Kiev."

Grigori tugged on the guy's collar and both the guy and Cal winced. In his time with Sokolov he'd already seen his share of beatings and even the occasional mutilation. Overall, the violence didn't bother him. What did was the dispassionate way his fellow gangsters went about their work.

Gangsters. The word irritated Cal, but there was no other word for it. He'd known what he was getting into from the moment he stepped on the plane over here, but the sheer reality of it wasn't any easier to swallow. He was used to violence as an expression of passion. Even in the military, when he was learning to kill, some part of him had known that if he was ever forced to take a life, it would be in the defense of his beloved country. But here, with these men, passion didn't matter. They were here to get paid. Violence was nothing more than a matter of business, a perfunctory exercise and means to an end. If only Grigori would get mad, call someone a bastard, yet only Sokolov was allowed to be angry on the job. Everyone else was expected to just get it over with.

"Thank you," Grigori said. "Good work as ever, Cal. Why don't you head back?"

"You don't need me?"

Grigori and the driver laughed. "We take two cars for reasons. Not needing you for this part."

Cal nodded and packed up his backpack.

"Wait," Grigori said. "Take laptop. You give it to other American. Tell him is for Armstrong."

He wanted to inquire further, but Cal knew he would get no answer. He retrieved his keys and edged past the driver on his way out of the man's home. Just as the door closed behind him, he heard a muffled shout and the undeniable sound of a punch landing on hard flesh.

✳ ✳ ✳

Matt opened the door to his hotel room; he raised an eyebrow but extended a hand. "Well, this is a surprise. Come on in."

Cal shook his buddy's hand and entered the room. It was the one proper hotel in Breznygrad, a dumpy little Holiday Inn sort of place with a terrible bar and restaurant off the lobby. Matt always stayed here when he was in town.

Matt took a pull off a pocket flask. "So, to what do I owe this honor?"

"It's three in the afternoon," Cal said quietly.

"Don't worry about it, I don't have nothing to do anyway."

Cal grunted. "Now you do." He threw his bag down on the bed and took out the laptop.

"What's that?"

"One of Sokolov's boys had it; real son of a bitch too. Looks like he's been selling to the Ukrainians."

Matt let out a low whistle. "What's on it?"

Cal had no idea, really; Sokolov had a brilliant system wherein he was the only person who ever had the full scope of his operations at any given point in time. Cal was only told what was absolutely necessary to get his job done; set up this system, find out if this guy is selling our secrets, get this server talking to that one; he never saw what was in the encrypted files. There were other guys he'd never met who were similarly in the dark about Cal's work, who sent him what was needed.

"I can't say, all I know is, it's for Armstrong."

Matt went chalk white. "Jesus," he muttered.

"I'm guessing this is more KGB than all that mob shit?"

"You know I couldn't tell you that if I wanted to."

"That explains why they caved in this poor bastard's skull over it."

"Fucking A; you want a drink? They do a decent margarita at that bar downstairs."

"I really ought not to; I need to get on back to my place ."

Matt pulled a wry grin. Cal had been seeing Polina for practically the whole time he'd been in Russia, and over time Matt's reaction had gone from angry insistence that they not see each other to grudging acceptance. It was clear that he was jealous of Cal, his better looks and less coarse personality.

"Well, you don't want to keep your wife waiting."

"She ain't my wife Matt, you know better; we haven't known each other that long. Wife, huh, first there is something called dating, then comes love, maybe, then comes commitment followed by

an engagement, then if all goes well and one or the other doesn't chicken out, there is a marriage. So, to set the record straight, we are just dating right now, okay."

Matt walked over to the dresser and opened a drawer, pulling out a pill bottle. He shook two into his palm and washed them down with the flask.

"I'll see you around, man." Cal uttered.

It occurred to him that leaving the computer in Matt's hands was a terrible idea.

❊ ❊ ❊

Cal drove toward his place, where Polina was surely waiting for him. They had started seeing each other officially less than a month after Cal moved to Breznygrad. He'd given her a door key and she would come and go at will.

At first, Cal had been too afraid to make any kind of official move. While there would be definite advantages to dating the boss's daughter, namely increased loyalty and proximity to power, it would also put his life in jeopardy. Sokolov didn't seem like the type to take kindly to a man breaking his daughter's heart. Everything about him reminded Cal of the stern, marble-faced dads who would chase him away from their girls in high school, were there even rumors of mutual interest.

Which is why it was such a shock when Sokolov called him into his office out at the mansion toward the end of his third month in Russia and did not break into a gangster version of a performance review. Instead, he broached the topic of Polina.

"So, Calvin Singer," he'd begun. "I have heard from Polina that you are fond of her."

Cal had broken into a cold sweat. He hadn't said anything to Polina at that point, but maybe she was psychic. "I mean, she's a very nice young woman, Mr. Sokolov."

His boss grunted. "She is huge pain in my ass. She went to school in France, learned nothing at all from what I can tell. Doesn't work, chases off every man. Paints pictures and does unspeakable things in Moscow, I am sure. She resents me because I never married her mother."

Cal had nodded along, mouth sewn shut. Now was not the time for pithy asides, although his interest was piqued as to what kind of "unspeakable things" his crush might have gotten up to.

"I have long been hoping she can find a nice man with whom to settle and make a family." Sokolov chuckled. "I guess you'll have to do."

Cal had opened and closed his mouth several times before finally managing to find the words. "Sir, I'm real honored you would think I'm worthy of your daughter, but I think there's been some misunderstanding."

Sokolov's attitude had darkened instantly. "What are you saying? Is my daughter not good enough for you? I know she is troublemaker, but why would you not want to make babies with her?"

"I'm not saying that at all, sir. I'm saying that I haven't really been involved with your daughter in any way. I'm saying I don't want to presume."

"Ah, well that is no trouble at all, I am sure she will have you, and I would be delighted to add you to family. Someone needs to take care of her; besides, she is wanting to go to America. I am sure you will go home some day?"

Cal hadn't thought of it. Wasn't a lot waiting for him stateside. "I suppose at some point I might."

"There we have it, you will marry Polina, and then we send you over to America and handle business there. It will be good for you. Come here, embrace me."

Cal had wanted to protest further, but Sokolov wasn't having it. Maybe he sensed his subordinate's tension and wanted to preempt it, or maybe he was just that blind. Either way, Cal had found himself crushed in the elderly but surprisingly strong man's arms, with promises that he would begin to court Miss Polina Popov as soon as possible.

Ever since then, she hadn't left him alone. Cal had worried that she'd be icy and withholding, but he was surprised at how affectionate she was. He still lived alone at his place but oft times Polina would slip in after midnight and slither into Cals bed absolutely stitch less. It was a glorious feeling to Cal, one he had never before felt. He would pretend to be fast asleep just so she would wake him by spooning and pressing her perky nipples against his back then kissing him in all the right places.

It was as if Polina had recognized that she had a good thing going here and was committed to keeping him around. She'd cook dinner for them both, not often but just enough to show that she could. Polina had a great love of nature, and she'd insist they take long trips out into forests and up mountains, bringing along pricey wine. Of course, she'd also expect him to accompany her to parties in Moscow, where she'd ply him with cocaine and show him off to her friends, who were all fascinated by the Southern gentleman turned gangster.

Polina would often bring up the topic of America, particularly the South. Her degree in France had apparently involved some sort of year abroad in Atlanta, where she had been charmed in every way. One excursion had taken her out to some plantation or other, where she had immediately fallen in love with the fantasy of rural living in what she saw as an American castle. Ever since then she'd had her heart set on one day living in a house like that, with a maid and a gardener, her days spent in peaceful luxury. The local Junior League would come over for iced sweet tea and petits fours, and she could regale them with tales of her life in Europe.

Cal saw little reason to disabuse her of her mistaken notions of Southern living. His experience had been one of the Upland South, well away from the fraught history of the antebellum period and fully rooted in the minor everyday horror of poverty in a town where the money had up and gone. Even down in Madison he hadn't been much of anything. Nonetheless, he told Polina story after story, embellishing or omitting as necessary. He was desperate to appear to her as a rough yet humble man of the dirt, wrongly persecuted and bravely working to make something of himself. He'd tell her about hunting for bucks, exaggerating the size of his quarry. He told her about all the barbecues down by the reservoir, spinning them into elegant luncheon parties and leaving out the parts where he was chased off the land for fighting with somebody's cancer-stricken uncle.

Sure enough, when Cal entered the door of his medium-sized but cheerful apartment, Polina was waiting for him. She would often spend days at a time lazing around the place, drinking tea and wine. There was no doubt they were being watched, but it seemed that Sokolov wasn't concerned with his daughter's "honor" so long as she wasn't being actively mistreated.

She ran up to him and gave him a hug. "My love. Have you been working?"

Cal nodded. He didn't feel like explaining, and she never felt like listening. Still, part of him wanted to tell someone about the effect the violence was having on him. "I had to visit someone. Grigori was there. It didn't go well."

Polina held her hands to her ears playfully. "No work-talk. I hate to hear of what awful things my papa asks of you."

"It wasn't me that had to do anything. It was Grigori."

"I don't want to know. Please do not make me hear of it. We can speak about something else."

Irritation gripped Cal. "You know, honey, sometimes a man just likes to come home from a hard day at work and share his troubles with somebody. I work really hard, and it wears on me."

"It doesn't matter, if we do not talk of it, then it is not real, not here." Polina snuggled against him.

Cal wanted to feel himself soften, but instead he just got more annoyed. "Well, it is real, and I don't want to just put it aside."

She put a hand on his face. "Please. I wait for you all day, why do you insist on talking of this? I don't want to know who my papa has killed, but you do not care, you make me think of it."

"Fine."

She snuggled up to him. "You should take better care of your girlfriend."

Polina kissed him on the mouth, and despite himself Cal give in. She wasn't often in the mood to stay home and just relax with him, but when she was, Polina could be quite the romantic. He picked her up—she weighed almost nothing—and carried her into the bedroom.

✧ ✧ ✧

Later that night, lying on his bed in the afterglow, Polina reached out and touched Cal's shoulder. "I am sorry it is so hard for you here. I do not wish to remain in Breznygrad either, but Papa has been insisting. He wants to keep me close, says I spend too much of his precious money in Moscow. Bastard man."

Polina's vulgarity toward her father never failed to shock Cal. "Well, I don't mind having you here."

She groaned. "You must ask Papa if you can go to America. Maybe you replace horrible Matthew; he is fat and unpleasant; he has no manners around a lady. Papa's people much rather speak to you, I am sure."

This again, Cal thought. It had long ago become clear to Cal that his primary value to both Sokolov and Polina was his connection to the American South. Polina would hint, with less subtlety than a native English speaker might, that she expected Cal to buy her one of those plantation mansions and deliver unto her all her dreams of ladyhood. Meanwhile, Sokolov would constantly interrogate him about Matt. Was he getting his money's worth? Did he need a man stateside who knew the region? Would there be anything Cal could do better than Matt?

What little integrity Cal had prevented him from speaking ill of his friend, but he secretly believed he could do whatever job Sokolov had given Matt and then some. Especially given how Matt had become increasingly erratic. Whenever they met up for dinner, the night would turn into a mess, as Matt alternately wept and shouted. Something was always wearing on him, be it his lack of romance or his fear at disappointing his bosses. And then Grigori would have to come by and collect them, shaking his head and muttering about keeping composure. The Russians partied hard, but—at least when it came to Sokolov's people—a level of decorum was expected. It was all well and good to take umbrage with some slight or another, but crying was an obvious sign of weakness and brawling was reserved for the tracksuit-clad youths who ran minor errands at Sokolov's request. There was a divide between the ex-military, ex-KGB guys who dealt with the serious national and overseas work and the felons and scoundrels who took care of the local stuff.

Matt, despite his fake-Mafia affectations, was firmly in the latter category. That didn't bode well for someone expected to carry sensitive documents back and forth to the United States.

"I think," Cal said to Polina, "that if your dad wants someone else doing Matt's thing, he'll let them know."

"And what is it he does?" She propped herself up on her elbows and looked at him.

Good question, Cal thought. "I thought you didn't want to talk about work."

"This is not work. This is my future. Our future."

The truth is, Cal wasn't sure what Matt did; his job, it seemed, was to simply take physical drives that Cal would sometimes load up with hundreds of gigabytes of .zip files and take them to America. Once there he'd get them where they needed to go. There were other guys who did the same, except they went to Baltimore and San Francisco. Cal saw the same names in the files over and over, but he was totally ignorant as to what any of it meant.

One name came up over and over: Armstrong. Cal thought back to the laptop he'd left with Matt. They were clearly engaging in espionage, if not outright treason, but if the CIA had picked him up at any given day and clamped a car battery to his nipples there wasn't shit Cal would be able to tell them. They'd have to catch six of Sokolov's guys to ever get even the faintest picture of what this simple "lumber exporter" was up to.

This was too much to explain to Polina, so Cal decided to make it as simple as possible. "He's a bag man, and if I may say so myself, I ain't no bag man."

"What do you mean, bag man?"

"I mean he's a delivery boy."

Polina laughed in the near-dark. "You are better than delivery boy. Does Papa not need computer man in Mississippi?"

Sokolov desperately needed a computer man or nine stateside. Cal was constantly irritated with the crappy security practices of his few counterparts in America. Nothing super important was done online, presumably because the feds were always watching. Still, more than once, Cal had received a big dump of vaguely sensitive materials that were poorly encrypted. It was mostly to do with local regulations on lumber usage, but sometimes it was sensitive information from state politicians clearly meant to be used as blackmail.

"Well, maybe," Cal said.

"You must speak to Papa," Polina said. "I insist. I cannot live in Breznygrad anymore. We must have our castle in the forest."

"It's not that easy."

"My papa might be pig, but he wants what is best for baby girl. You will go speak to him. I demand it."

Cal stared at the ceiling, cursing his lover. Who would have thought dating a hot, rich, college-educated Russian girl would be so hard? If only Sokolov wasn't so desperate to marry her off. Then he could have had his pick of the locals and been happier for it.

✦ ✦ ✦

For some reason Sokolov was working out of the one strip club in Breznygrad. Like everything else in the town, it was both rundown and somehow related to Sokolov's business. To him, espionage and politicking were his true passions. Everything else—the gigantic sawmill, the extortion racket, the gangs of youths who sold tiny bags of various powders on the street corners—was nothing more than funding his network of information smuggling.

Cal wound his way around the stages and through the dressing area to the back office and knocked on the door. Sokolov shouted *"Da!"* from inside and Cal entered to see his boss, clad in a suit as ever, sweating in a tiny, hellishly warm office. Cal sidled up next to Grigori, who was also packed into the room, giving him a small nod.

"Ah, it is Calvin Singer," Sokolov said. He took out a huge handkerchief and mopped his brow. "Why do you come to see me?"

"Well, sir, I've been speaking to Polina."

"My darling. How is she?"

"We're doing just fine, sir, thanks for asking." Now that he was going, Cal knew he couldn't stop or else he'd lose his nerve. "What I was wondering, or I should say what we were wondering, is if there's any work for me in the States? You see, she's got her heart set on moving back to my neck of the woods, and well, I was thinking I wouldn't mind seeing home either. Also, to be honest with you, your guys over there aren't worth whatever you're paying them."

Sokolov was quiet for a while. Finally, he gave out a big sigh. "I know these boys in America are awful. That is why I hire you here. That is why I have you date Polina. I hoped to send you back."

Cal felt a bit of delight that quickly faded into confusion. "What do you mean, had me date Polina?"

"I know she is quite fond of you, but honestly I cannot bear to have her here. She is always coming to me; she is always demanding. If she is gone, then she will call me and ask for money. If she is here, then she is demanding to see me. But if she has a husband, he can give her children. She can be far away, and I can do my work."

For a moment Cal found his boss to be very insensitive to his child, but he had to admit that Polina demanded quite a bit of attention. "So, does that mean you want us to move?"

"I suppose no time like present." He turned to Grigori and spoke in Russian. "Matty boy is in town. I will put you on flight back with him. We will need you in Mississippi. You can find big house for my beautiful daughter. You will then come back and marry her and be my Southern guy. This is good?"

The thought of marrying Polina filled Cal with equal dread and pleasure. When he came here, marriage was the last thing on his mind, and now he kicked himself for not expecting this. She would surely be a handful, but she was truly beautiful and an excellent companion in her own way. Who was Cal to complain about his hot, new wife? A year before he'd been a security guard, and now look at him. Already, for the first time ever, he was looking forward to his next high school reunion.

"Mr. Sokolov, nothing would make me happier."

✿ ✿ ✿

Of course, Polina was ecstatic when he told her. Cal took her out to Osteria Mario a very nice white tablecloth Italian restaurant in Moscow and then onto the river for a short tour. She cried when he got down on one knee and pulled out the ring, and the whole boat clapped for them and passed out complimentary champagne. It was like something out of a movie. For some wild reason he had expected her to reject him, to laugh or, worse, frown and ask why the ring wasn't bigger. But it seemed that she wasn't a gold digger, just ambitious. It was a relief.

Getting the ring had been the hard part. Grigori had taken him out to find one, not in Breznygrad of course. They had gone to three places to find one that matched what little Cal knew of Polina's taste. It was simple, but the square cut diamond was quite large. He had the money for it, but it would be a hell of a dent.

To Cal's surprise, when the time came to pay Grigori pulled out a massive wad of rubles.

"What are you doing?" Cal asked.

Grigori chuckled. "Boss say it's all his money anyway. Wants Polina to say yes."

"So, there are perks to marrying the boss's daughter."

"Wait and see. Christmas will be good to you."

Being engaged did wonders for Polina. Her dark moods shortened, and in their place came endless talk of what kind of home she wished to live in. She would spend every waking hour regaling Cal with visions of wide-plank floors and ornate moldings, breezy verandas and spacious windows. She redoubled her efforts at improving her English, spent hours poring over recipe books, and watched everything from *To Kill a Mockingbird* to *Fried Green Tomatoes*.

Cal didn't have the heart to tell her that, while her father had paid for the ring, he very much doubted it would be easy for a Russian mobster to purchase a multimillion-dollar home for his son-in-law. Not to mention that Sokolov had specified that he be near Jackson. Cal was also very aware that buying a house way out in the sticks was neither a good use of funds nor practical for a commute.

He wondered if he could approach Sokolov on his next visit for an advance on his salary. Would Sokolov agree? After all, any mortgage would require verification of employment and a paper trail as to where such a large sum of cash came from. Could Sokolov's firm provide legitimate employment records to support him? It would at least require a substantial down payment. His previous employment records surely would not hold water for savings of this magnitude. Even if Sokolov out and out gave him a bag of cash, how could he manage to use it for the down payment or full purchase for that matter with no formal acquisition papers?

Nevertheless, he resolved to find her something brand new. His earning potential was guaranteed to go up, anyway

"She asks a lot," he told Matt the night before they were set to go back to America. Matt had insisted they share a beer at the hotel bar for good luck. "But have you seen her? It's worth it."

Matt shook his head, forlorn. "You get all the breaks, kid. Me, I'm scrounging up seconds over here." He looked across the room at an older, heavier woman.

"I got lucky. Ain't a single thing more to it. Besides, she makes a lot of demands."

"You know how happy I'd be to take orders from a woman like that?"

"You say that now. Spend a day with her, see what you say."

"Yeah, yeah. I'm happy for you, though," Matt said. He raised his drink. "No jealousy between comrades."

Cal laughed and clinked his glass against Matt's. "None at all, buddy. We better pack it in."

Matt agreed, and they shook hands before parting ways. Cal had offered him a chance to stay at his place so they could leave together come morning, but Matt refused on account of his snoring and a very particular morning ritual.

✻✻✻

Cal was in an altogether good mood, if slightly hungover, when the car showed up the next morning to take him to the airport, driven by that same silent driver whose name he'd never known. Feeling chipper, he decided to finally try to make conversation.

"Say there, buddy. What's your name?"

The man looked in the rearview mirror and said nothing. Instead of turning onto the main road toward the highway, he instead went down a side road Cal didn't recognize.

"Is this a shortcut?" Cal asked. "Flight's in about two hours, pal."

His driver still didn't respond, and panic filled him. Had he been duped? But then he saw Sokolov's mansion pull into view as the car wound its way through a back road, down the driveway, and pulled up in front of Matt's hotel.

"Volgin," the driver said.

"What's that?"

"Name. Volgin." He opened the door. "Sokolov is waiting."

"Aren't we here to pick up Matt?"

Volgin turned around and shook his head.

❖ ❖ ❖

Nothing could have prepared Cal for the scene in Matt's room. The first thing that hit him was the smell. As soon as the door opened, the unmistakable scent of vomit assailed his nostrils. Furniture was upended, the mirror was shattered, and sure enough, vomit pooled in odious puddles on the rug. And on the bed lay Matt, with Sokolov and Grigori looming over him.

"Ah, Calvin Singer," Sokolov said. He grinned, and his voice was jovial, but his skin was pale, and taut with rage. "The other American joins us. We are honored."

"Hi," Cal said. He couldn't get more out, from both disgust and fear. A trickle of something yellow dribbled out of Matt's mouth.

Sokolov gestured at the bed. "So, as you see, your friend is in no state to fly. He is in very bad shape. It seems he think, well, if I am to fly, I should become very drunk. Yes, this is a good idea."

"I don't imagine he's going to make it through customs."

Grigori frowned, but Sokolov threw his head back in fake laughter. "I don't imagine he will be able to walk, let alone pass security check. So, I ask you, did you have something to do with this? My daughter, she says you two go out last night."

Cal seized up. "Mr. Sokolov, I swear on my life this man was upright when I left him last night. We each had a beer and talked about how much we wanted to go back to the States. There wasn't a single thing more to it, and I am just as shocked as you are to see him like this."

"Really? That is difficult to believe."

Fear turned to anger, and Cal snapped. "You calling me a liar?"

Grigori took a few steps toward Cal. "Remember what I tell you when we meet," he said softly. "Do not be readying for a fight."

The Russian was huge and smelled of aftershave. Cal swallowed his rage and turned back toward his boss. "Mr. Sokolov, I give you my most solemn oath that Matthew Hussy was in good working order the last time I saw him. Look at me—if I were the cause, why am I not just as drunk? Sir, we had one beer together before parting for the night. Whatever he got up to in here was well after I was at home, sleeping beside your daughter, and preparing to leave on your orders."

Sokolov took two huge breaths. "Fine. It is too late now. Now you must do job of two."

"I do?"

"You will take package with you to Mississippi. You will make extra trip to Atlanta. We will tell you where and who to meet. That is that."

"Yes, sir," Cal said. He knew better than to argue.

Sokolov rooted through Matt's half-packed bag and pulled out three hard drives. "Why does he have three drive?"

Cal's heart sank. "He must have screwed it up, I told him how to do it, and he apparently couldn't follow the instructions."

Sokolov raised an eyebrow. "You told him?* Look at him. Do you think he can do anything? He is useless." He threw the drives to Cal, who caught them. "Fix it. Now."

Sweating, Cal grabbed Matt's laptop off the desk. It was password protected, but that had never stopped him before. He had a feeling that Matt hadn't made any effort to harden his system, and as he effortlessly cracked through the encryption and populated the contents of the drives, he realized he was correct. Sokolov was right. Matt was useless, and Cal never should have trusted him for anything.

It turned out the only reason Matt needed three drives was simple laziness. The files were too big when put into one .rar file to transfer at once, so instead the dope had cut them into three and loaded them all at the same time instead of doing it one at a time. The worst part, besides the fact that it wasn't done right and probably corrupted some of the files, is that his method probably took longer.

Minutes turned into hours, but finally they were done. Just as the files finished, Matt woke up.

"What's that?" He looked around him and saw Cal first. "Oh, hey, man. What are you doing in my room?" He smiled, but that vanished as he saw Grigori and Sokolov looming over him.

"Volgin," Sokolov said. "Take Cal. Get him new flight."

Volgin's hand rested on Cal's shoulder and guided him out of the room, clutching the single hard drive. Cal looked over his shoulder. The last thing he saw before the door closed was Matt's pleading gaze.

So, it was up to Volgin to fill Cal in on the way to the airport. The driver was, hands down, the worst conversationalist Cal had ever met, all gruff asides and short sentences.

"Boss tells me you are from Jackson Mississippi," Volgin had said. His droopy eyes locked with Cal's in the rearview mirror. There was an unsettling sense of knowledge in them.

"Well, not exactly," Cal had said. "I lived there. With … ," and then the image of Matt's last gaze returned, unbidden. "What are they going to do to him?"

Volgin ignored the question. "Good that you are from Jackson. Makes it easier." He had passed Cal a business card. "Memorize this, then destroy it before you get on the plane."

"What are you expecting me to do? I've never done this before, not really. And now my friend is back there. Please tell me what they're going to do."

"Do you really want to know? Or do you ask for polite?"

"I do, I swear to you. I do not want any harm to come to Matt. He's an idiot sometimes, but not a bad person."

Volgin had grunted and said no more. When they arrived at the airport, he pulled the car to the curb and got out. He grabbed Cal's hastily packed suitcase and the precious bag of drives and shoved them into the American's arms.

"If really friends, then will not tell you anything. Kinder that way."

Cal had stared at the business card for a full hour before tearing it into as many tiny pieces as his fingers could grab and dribbling it out the car window as they approached the airport, forcing himself not to think of Matt, to ignore the horror now resting deep in his mind. The address he knew. By some miracle or trick of fate it was the same building he'd worked security for when he lived there.

Or maybe it wasn't coincidence at all. Maybe the whole thing, for years before he was aware of it, had been an audition, an extended interview. Maybe Matt had been watching him, pulled strings to get him the job at the office building in the first place. But then wouldn't they have given him a technical position?

The name on the card: Adam Ostelot. Titles: President, Chief Operations Officer. Company: Revolver Solutions.

So, this seems legit Cal thought, but is it?

Five

*I*t was bittersweet to be back in Jackson. There had been a time when Cal wanted nothing more than to never see Mississippi ever again, to fly away to some glorious future and flip off the whole damn state as he passed. But after everything that he'd gone through the last few months, he had to admit there was something soothing about the sight of that old low-rise office building.

They'd let him twist for a few days. Cal was living out of the ground floor of a cheap motel on the outskirts of town, watching reruns of all the *Rocky* and *Rambo* movies he could find and eating vending machine bags of stale potato chips. Every time he heard a car rumble into the parking lot, he flew to the window and peeked out. Invariably it was either some broke family with barefoot kids or a middle-aged man accompanied by a scantily clad, heavily made-up young woman. Still, Cal expected at every moment to be shot, for someone to barge into his room guns blazing and relieve him of the surely expensive burden of the drives. He took to sleeping with a pistol under his pillow barely catching more than an hour's sleep every night.

But no one ever came. The Russians were either waiting for the right moment to give him further instructions, or they were debating whether to kill him and start the Mississippi operation from scratch. Either way, Cal had been wishing they'd get it over with. He'd packed and repacked his suitcase, ready to jump ship and hit the road at any time. It was only the knowledge of his responsibility to Polina that kept him from running and reassured him that death probably wasn't in his immediate future.

With nothing better to do, he'd spent his days cruising real estate websites, looking for their new home. Rehearsing over and over in his head what he would ask Sokolov to do for him. Convinced himself that Sokolov was a reasonable man and could surely see for himself that Cal couldn't afford such a home without financial assistance. Sokolov had purchased the wedding ring, but would he spring for the house of Polina's dreams as well and if so, how would he accomplish that? It quickly became clear that Polina's expectations were unreasonable at best. There were no plantation homes near Jackson that looked remotely livable. All of them were either too far away, too rundown, or because they were attached to several thousand farm acres, were just far too expensive and unpractical to even come close to delivering her fantasy. Even the replica homes, the ones built in an antebellum style but far more recently, were at the top of Cal's price point. The thought of living in a house with a name, an old storied place with history and acres of land, was laughable. What would he tell his few friends and family of how he had acquired the wealth that allowed him to buy such a place? He knew there would be a lot of questions, questions that he would have to begin fabricating lies to answer. Although his paycheck was bigger than anything he had ever imagined, he had no decent credit at the banks, no long-standing relationship that might garner him a pass on credit history. They'd have to save up for a few years and either build new or sink their cash into one of the historic ones, with a substantial mortgage; besides, Polina had a huge appetite for spending and was draining money from their joint account like rain through a screen door. Without the help of her father, Cal could not fathom how he could possibly pull it off.

Polina had been sending him emails damn near every night, too. They were invariably filled with romantic visions and an almost palpable excitement at the thought of their new life. Her descriptions of the ideal home were getting even more detailed, and with each new email Cal grew more and more concerned. Her rising expectations coupled with the falling prospects were, he already knew, a recipe for disaster. But he could not find the words to dissuade her of her expectations, especially not after a full year of feeding her his half-truths. He found himself in an increasingly tense situation, with no sign of relief.

Then one afternoon, out of the blue, he got a text message from an unknown number. *Go to Revolver tomorrow, 2 PM. Do not answer.*

The message was exceedingly terse, but nonetheless relief washed over Cal in an awesome wave. They were not through with him, not yet. He had gotten the barest amount of information, and with it a similar amount of peace of mind. He could go back to finding a house later.

It was the lack of information that was really driving him crazy, or at least crazier than usual. The connection between Jackson and Russia had not been clear whenever Cal headed out with Matt for the "interview," as Cal now liked to think of it. His time in Russia hadn't exactly cast light on it either. He'd served as a simple functionary, doing a specific handful of tasks that obfuscated the greater plans of his boss.

The flight had been uneventful, as had the drive to the motel, and here he was, stepping through the doors of his old and now new workplace, dressed in slacks and a blazer, holding shady Russian hard drives and approaching the familiar figure seated behind the security desk.

JD spoke without looking up. "Sign in, please."

"Hello, JD," Cal said, with as much honey in his voice as he could muster.

JD glanced up and wheeled his chair back an inch. He looked like he'd seen someone come back from the dead. "Well, I'll be damned. What the hell are you doing here? I ain't giving you your job back, if that's what you're angling for. A man walks out on me, he can stay gone."

"Not at all, JD," Cal said, sweetening his voice even more. "See, I've had a bit of a change in fortune. Made some new friends and scored a new position that takes advantage of my talents."

"What talents? Being a violent, no-good, insubordinate, perpetually late bag of lazy bones?"

"Oh, JD. I'd explain it to you, but I don't think you've got what it takes to get on with what I do for a living."

"Watch your mouth, boy. You might have hoodwinked some poor sap into giving you a job, but if it was up to me, you'd never work around these parts again. You're a worthless loser and an imbecile."

Cal leaned in and spoke softly. The anger mixed with pride was so lovely, so invigorating, he had to exert more self-control than he had in years. "I'm afraid my fighting days are behind me, JD. I got me a nice fiancée, and I'm eager to bring her round and show her the place. Wouldn't do for an upstanding member of the community to be brawling all over the place, you understand."

"Well. Good to know."

"But don't you ever forget for a moment who I am. I've taken down bigger guys for less than your little speech just now. You don't watch how you speak, and you might find yourself getting a better view of who I truly am than you ever wanted. We clear, JD?"

"You're a real son of a bitch."

"And you'd do well to keep that in mind." Cal stood up to his full, considerable height. "Now, I'm looking for Revolver Solutions. You care to direct me?"

JD mumbled the floor and suite number. "You're on six. Suite D. Only one up there, anyway."

Cal was taken aback for a moment. "I don't remember that floor having much of anything when I was here. They must have recently moved in, I mean since I've been gone?"

"Shows what you know. They've been there the whole time."

Cal cast back his memory. Was there ever an occupied office up there? He remembered some desks, a few telephones and older model computers but that was about it. Nothing was ever left turned on and the telephones never rang when he was making his rounds. Then again, he'd always been the third-shift guy and had assumed that this was furniture left over from some firm that had simply closed up shop one day and walked out leaving everything behind as many do.

Cal slapped the desk in front of him. "Mighty obliged, JD. Remember what I said. I'll be seeing you around, seeing as I work here and all."

It was all Cal could do not to whoop for victory in the elevator. That little interaction with JD seemed to make it all worth it, all the trouble, the violent Russians, the questionable legality of his position, even whatever grim fate Matt had gotten himself into. It was a taste of respect, the respect he was so deeply owed and had given so much up for.

And besides, hadn't Matt gotten himself into this? Wasn't it his fault, with all the drinking and drugs, the whoring and carousing? He'd taken on a dangerous, important role for dangerous, important people, and slipped down so far that there was no redeeming him. Anyone else would have shit-canned him a long time ago, and from there it would be a slow slide into alcoholism, depression, and homelessness. He'd probably have wound up hanging himself from the ceiling in some godforsaken Comfort Inn one day. No, if anything the Russians' methods would be a mercy. Better quick and clean than slow and dirty.

The elevator spat Cal out on the sixth floor, and for a moment he just stood and stared at the surroundings.

When he'd worked there, there had been some remodeling this floor, 30but he'd never seen even one office worker come through.

And now, over a year later, this part of the area still looked uninhabited: shabby, dirty, and with building materials scattered all down the corridor. Well, at this point it wasn't as much of a surprise. The place had never been in the absolute best shape, and besides, the Russians choosing cheap, nondescript locations for their operations was standard operating procedure at that point. It probably would have been a bigger surprise if it was shining clean and utterly modern.

Cal shrugged and turned down the hall. No point in overthinking it. He couldn't imagine the Russians would benefit from having a bunch of unrelated fellows sweeping in and out at every turn.

Revolver Solutions was behind a frosted glass door down a side corridor. Cal reached out and opened it. Despite himself, he let out a gasp. The place was a wreck.

Only a handful of people were there, seated at cheap desks. There were at least four computers for each human, and thick bands of cables snaked all over the cheap indoor-outdoor carpet. One of the walls was down, exposing the structure of the building, and even more cables wound their way up it.

"Are you Cal?"

A dumpy young woman with neon-green hair sat at the nearest desk, her feet on the desk.

"I'm here to see Adam Ostelot?" Cal said uncertainly. Was this all a practical joke?

"Ah, thought so," said the young woman. "I'm Meryl. Nice to meet you. I'm the secretary. You need to fax something, ask me. I'm the only one who can get the damn thing to work."

"Thanks. Is Mr. Ostelot here?"

Meryl pitched her head back. "Hey, Adam! Your two o'clock is here."

A blond man turned around and walked over, deliberately. He wore a clean, expensive suit that belied the disorder of his surroundings. Cal couldn't help but notice he was exceedingly well groomed, and handsome to boot.

"Hello," Cal said, holding out a hand. "I'm Calvin Singer. It's an absolute pleasure to meet you. I can't tell you how pleased I am to be here."

Adam looked down at the bag Cal was still clutching. "You're late." He had a perfect television anchor voice. Too perfect.

"I'm terribly sorry. I have a bad habit of tardiness. You'd think the Army would have beat it out of me, but I'm afraid some things are just too deep to shake loose."

"Cut the charm school act," Adam said. He clipped the ends of his words. "You're late. Don't be."

"Sure thing, Mr. Ostelot."

"What did I just say?"

Cal's blood spiked with irritation, and he couldn't stop himself from speaking. "Sorry, I tried to be polite, Adam. Thought maybe you'd appreciate it."

"Are you angry, Calvin Singer? You look like you might be. Or do you simply love to waste time?"

Cal swallowed down as much of his anger as he could. "I don't like interrogations."

"Oh, but I do," Adam said. He finally cracked the smallest of grins. "Interrogation used to be my specialty. Is it Calvin? Or Cal? Perhaps Mr. Singer?"

"Cal is good."

"I know who you are, Cal. I wonder if you know who I am, and how important this thing you have been asked to do is."

Cal threw his hands up. The bag waved uselessly. "I would, if somebody opened their damn mouth and told me. I know what I learned from …." He paused, unsure how freely he could speak. "I know what the guy who hired me told me. I don't know a whole lot else, about why I'm here, about Revolver, and especially not about you."

Adam rested a finger on his bottom lip. "You know why I named this place Revolver?" he asked. "It's because I've always loved cowboys. John Wayne, Eastwood. *3:10 to Yuma* is my favorite film. The original, not the godawful remake. The lawman and the thief, they both are men of integrity. They are exactly what they appear to be and do not use lies and trickery. In the days of the Old West, men were men, and you were only as good as your shooting arm."

"I believe that everyone should be who they are," Adam continued. "And if they refuse to let that show, then they ought to be forced to. If it takes pain, or pressure, then I will apply it as needed. I know where you came from, and I know how you've been spending your time. I wouldn't have consented to take you on if I wasn't looking for a mean son of a bitch who knew his place. So, don't put on a voice when you're speaking to me, and we'll get along just fine, got it?"

It was quiet for a moment. Everyone working ignored them, kept at their tasks. There was a popping sound, and Cal turned to see Meryl chewing bubblegum, huge headphones blocking out any sound.

"I don't like it when you say I know my place," Cal said. "Makes me sound unambitious. I got dreams too, you know, same as any other man."

Adam smiled, for real this time. "I know you do, Cal, and you're living them! That's how I'm sure you know your place. Come on, I'll show you around. But first, let me have the bag."

Cal had forgotten he was holding his briefcase containing the single drive he'd created just before leaving Matt's room. He handed it to Adam who took it to the nearest computer, plugged it in, and with a few keystrokes effortlessly decrypted the files. Cal was impressed despite himself. He'd taken Adam to be a managerial type, not somebody with technical knowledge.

"So, is this where Matt was taking all them damn drives?"

Adam held up a hand. "Please, Cal, let me impress upon you the need for discretion. This company is, for all intents and purposes, almost entirely separate from your previous employer. We're contractors, you see, and our primary client is an American importer of lumber. What affiliations they may have to your previous employer, I really couldn't comment on."

Cal nodded. Adam seemed a bit terse but not unintelligent. He'd underestimated this guy.

"So, are you my boss, now?"

Adam looked at him out of the corner of his eye. "I sign your check; well, technically, I approve your direct deposit."

"That doesn't answer my question."

"You'll have to learn to love the answers you get. Looks like everything is here."

Cal grunted consent. "I know what I'm doing."

"That was never in doubt. Wouldn't have hired you if I didn't." He stood up and walked Cal through the tangle of desks. "You'll have to forgive the mess. Most of our people work remotely, so we don't really spruce up the place. When you must come in, I'll let you know, but most of your work will be done either through Secure Shell on our servers, or preferably entirely offline. You'll be issued a laptop."

The idea of having all his work done on a machine that would surely be shot through with spyware aggravated Cal, but he also understood why it was necessary. Still, he couldn't help but wish they'd have put a bit more effort into making this place look good. He'd been hoping for an office, something with a bit of class that would make him feel like a big shot. To learn he'd be sitting in his house logging in from afar was a letdown to say the least. And what was the deal with that secretary?

"Who all works here?" Cal asked. "That receptionist doesn't seem like much."

"A distant relative of our client." The tension in Adam's voice betrayed his irritation with her. "Nepotism. I'm sure you under-stand." He led Cal down a side hallway and to a door with a combination lock. He briskly typed in a few numbers, then held his thumb to a scanner. "You'll find this room more than makes up for what's out there."

He opened the door, and Cal let out a low whistle. It was a server room, the largest he'd seen since leaving the military. The air was freezing, no doubt to preserve the racks and racks of computers, modems, and storage drives that lived inside. Cal tried to do the math in his head, to figure out how much all of this would cost. He stopped when he got to eight digits.

"I don't need to tell you what this is, of course."

"No sir," Cal said. "Damn, that's a lot of hardware."

"We know where to put the money, when we need to. Our client is a notorious cheapskate, but we get the job done." Adam chuckled. "As for who works here, mostly you and me. A few techs to maintain the stuff."

"That's it? Seems like a skeleton crew."

"What do you think we do here, Cal?"

"Mail-order bride scams? Sell people's credit card numbers? Find new and exciting ways to increase efficiency at sawmills?"

Adam groaned. "I'm not a kind man, but just this once I'll make an exception. Do you really want to know what's going on, Cal?"

Cal thought about Adam's swagger and the speech he gave about integrity. Wasn't exactly Cal's favorite way to be, and if anything, it turned him off. But he couldn't help but see Adam as a challenge, and one that he needed to answer. So, he decided, freezing his balls off in the server room, to tell the truth.

"I don't have a choice," he said. "I'm already in with the … client's daughter, and I don't have any other job prospects. And I sure as shit ain't going back to walking the halls of this place with a flashlight, calling out 'All clear.' So, if you got something, you need to clue me in."

"That's the first intelligent thing you've said since you got here," Adam said. He closed the door and herded Cal back toward the front. "I'll tell you what. You weren't entrusted with the details of our client's operations. So, how's about I pick you up tomorrow, and I show you what we really do?"

"And now you're going to jump me into the gang?"

"In a manner of speaking, yes. Where are you staying?"

Cal told him, and Adam clucked his tongue, shaking his head.

"Don't be such a cheapskate. Your wife won't be. You should learn how to spend what you have, considering you're coming up in the world. Stay at the Hilton."

"Bit rich for my blood."

"You'll expense it. Remember who signs your checks now."

"Thought it was direct deposit."

"I'd advise you to shut your mouth, unless you want me to take a liking to you."

❖ ❖ ❖

The car showed up at 12:20 p.m., ten minutes before their agreed-upon time. Cal swore loudly and rushed to find his tie pin. He was angry at himself for being surprised by the call. Hadn't Adam made it clear that punctuality was of the utmost importance now?

If nothing else, the Hilton was a much nicer place to stay. Cal hadn't ever slept on sheets so fine, or a bed so luxuriously soft. He got room service and damn near cleared out the minibar, stretching his considerable length along the mattress as he watched a pay-per-view movie, the bedspread littered with peanut wrappers and tiny emptied bottles.

Learn how to spend, Adam had told him. Well, he was trying, wasn't he? Cal had never had much, all things considered.

89

He'd grown up with a bunch of no-count fools in coal country, then transitioned into his brief military stint and the sharp fall off into nomadic underemployment that came with his discharge. Money had always been tight, and even the year of decent pay under Sokolov hadn't been enough to shake his habit of hoarding money and pinching pennies. He had anticipated that with a windfall he would be like all his neighbors back in Kentucky who stumbled onto money and immediately blew it all on a lifted truck and the biggest television they could fit in their living rooms. That fear had resulted in an overcorrection the other way and an unfortunate habit of not spending at all. Before Matt had spirited him away to Breznygrad, his one vice had been their occasional trips to the bar. But now, with his increase in fortune, there was a corresponding expectation in lifestyle. After all, he would soon be a married man.

A stab of panic hit him as he thought of Polina. There was a secondary expectation here. After checking in at the Hilton, he'd found a listing for a nice, new five-bedroom, three and a half bath, lake front in what looked like a pleasant subdivision over in Lake Caroline. It was the kind of place he'd have killed to live in back when he was swatting water bugs in the family shithole back in Kentucky. He knew Polina would be disappointed, but from the listing it was a legitimately nice place to live, and he felt that he could sell her on the idea of at least settling down for a bit while they built their dream.

He shot off a text message to the real estate agent and finally pinned his tie into place as his phone rang again. Cal silenced it and ran to the elevator.

Outside the front doors a black Town Car was waiting for him. The driver popped out and opened the door, and Cal mumbled his thanks, annoyed that he'd have to tip the guy.

"You're late," Adam said. He was in the rear passenger seat, one leg crossed over the other. On the seat next to him was a leather briefcase.

"It's not even 12:30 yet."

"I know. It's a joke. Lighten up, will you?" Adam chuckled. "I need to keep you sharp."

"Appreciate it." Cal said. It was impossible to keep an edge of sarcasm out of his voice. "Where are we headed?"

"To the office of one of our client's clients," Adam said. "How did you like the Hilton?"

"Much better."

"Did you raid the minibar?"

"Should I not have?"

"I'd be insulted if you didn't," Adam said. "The people we're going to meet, they don't like cheapskates. They're not opposed to frugality per se, but they think of money in terms of what it can do. Incidental, personal expenditure should no longer be on your mind, Cal."

"That's going to be a hard habit to break, I'm afraid."

"I've been to your hometown; I don't blame you, it's a real piece of work, if you don't mind me saying. How's the house hunt going?"

"How do you know about that?"

"Let me try this a different way. You would describe what we do as intelligence, would you not, Cal? I assume you've realized that carrying data across national borders is an unusual endeavor. If that's the case, then you should assume that anything you know, we know. So, in the spirit of openness, how's the house hunt going?"

"She wants to live on an antebellum plantation. Can you believe it? I don't have the heart to tell her no."

Adam chewed this news over in silence for a moment. "Don't disappoint Sokolov."

"Now he's Sokolov again?"

"We're here. If you need me to say more, then you're too stupid to work for us anyway, Calvin Singer."

"You said both my names. That's a Russian thing. Thought I should ask, in the spirit of openness."

Adam turned his icy gaze on Cal. "Dual citizenship." He laughed. "We recruit from every level of Russian intelligence. Sometimes we even get guys on loan from Putin's inner circle. It's a shame about how fragmented things are now, what with the need to maintain a veneer of democracy. But still, we get the job done."

"Great English. I mean, you speak good English."

"Training. And a lot of talent. You're not down in the slums anymore, Calvin Singer."

* * *

The Town Car had taken them a few miles out of Jackson through the gates of a country club. Cal gave a low whistle as he looked at the clubhouse. Well, if Polina wanted a plantation home, maybe she could live here.

The driver let them out, and Adam led him through the atrium, past waiters and butlers in uniforms who nodded their heads and addressed Adam as *Mr. Ostelot.* If he wasn't a member, he must surely come here often enough. They wound their way through the halls and into a private party room that could seat fifty comfortably. A single man sat waiting for them at a twelve-seat table in the far corner. He was an older, balding guy in golf attire, grassy cleats and all.

"Adam, you Soviet bastard," the balding man said. His voice boomed. "How's business?"

Adam put the briefcase down on the table and slid it over. "See for yourself."

The balding man opened it up and smiled. "They don't pay you enough." He held out a hand toward Cal. "Pleasure to meet you. You'll forgive me if I don't give you my name. I don't know you from Adam." He chuckled at his own joke.

Adam took a chair and motioned for Cal to sit. "This is Calvin Singer. You'll be seeing more of him. He's Matthew Hussy's replacement."

"About damn time they got rid of that worthless son of a bitch. You want a Diet Coke? Shrimp cocktail?"

"No, I'm fine," Cal said. "Look, I'm sorry to be difficult, but I'm afraid I'm plumb confused here. You said you knew Matt? He is an old friend of mine, a drinking buddy so to speak. If you could, I'd appreciate you letting me know exactly what's going on, or else I'm afraid I'll be just as worthless to you as he was."

The balding man looked at Cal like he was a space alien, then turned to Adam. "Is he always like this, or should I be flattered?"

"I'm trying to teach him not to blow smoke up asses," Adam said. "Give him time."

"Well, now listen here, Cal. You ever heard of a political action committee, PAC for short?"

Cal swallowed. "I'm familiar with the term. They advocate for candidates and issues that concern voters, correct?"

"They're a damn bribing scheme is what they are," said the balding man. His impatience was mounting. "We're all friends here, let's call it what it is. And I happen to run a damn good one. Now, your Russian friend here has been helping us out in more ways than one. Carrying us all kinds of good stuff. But see, we need a nice, unsuspicious American to stop by and deliver now and again. Real easy, one that your friend Matt couldn't seem to manage. Bastard was drunk half the time, and late the other half."

Cal stared for a moment. "Just tell me what kind of information I'm passing here?"

The balding man bellowed with laughter, and Adam managed a small grin.

"He's marrying the big man's daughter," Adam said. "All right, Calvin Singer. I can't have you running around the American South not knowing how valuable you are." He grabbed a nearby pitcher of water and poured some for Cal.

"Listen up," Adam said. "The drives you've been carrying around contain all kinds of useful information. Some of it is financial instruments. Some of it is detailed schematics of logging equipment. Some of it has to do with the friendly American agents who seek to plunge my country back to the age of the tsar."

"If anyone asks, I didn't hear none of that," the balding man chuckled.

"And some of it is the kind of information that's useful to political candidates in the American South. See, the Russian state would like to have some … friendly faces in the U.S. government. So, we give them a hand. Sometimes that means we have to offer a gift, and sometimes they reach out to us. The light stuff, the matters that pertain to voter rolls and such, we can do that here. From Revolver. Which you'll be helping with."

Cal swallowed. "And the rest?"

"Oh, the rest can be anything from deeds to Russian land, all the way to some terribly compromising photos that may or may not have been produced at the behest of our government. Some are Democrats, some Republicans. We don't judge, you see. Russia did away with multiple parties when Lenin delivered us from the Romanov scum and purged the revisionists of the White Army. Perhaps one day you will be so enlightened."

"I haven't voted in years," Cal said stupidly.

"Now, say some friendly land developer comes to Moscow, he likes watching pretty girls relieve themselves. We like watching him watch. Now we have a video that he has a vested interest in not being seen. And it's a lot easier and safer to carry, say, a digital copy of that tape in person, you see. Then split those files up and get them where they need to go."

"What's in the case?"

"Above your pay grade, son," said the balding man.

"Now this is the part," Adam said, "where I should ask you if you're okay with this. But you are okay with it, aren't you Cal? Or would you like to explain to Polina Popov's father that you're a fucking coward?"

There was nothing he could say. "Now it was real. He had kidded himself sometimes that the files were really about lumber and 'investments,' but now, now he knew beyond any shadow of doubt he was a traitor, guilty of treason and election tampering. If they caught him now, his ass would be in the slinger, crossbar hotel for life, maybe worse, no doubt about it.

His text message notification went off. The real estate agent got back to him. *Can you go view it this evening?*

So, Cal nodded. It was easier to just go along with it. Besides, what did America ever do for poor old Calvin Singer except deal him a losing hand anyway?

Six

Cal signed his name by the X with a little extra flourish, relishing the most important autograph he'd ever give a document.

"Congratulations," said the real estate agent. "You're a homeowner, or at least you will be in a few days when we do the closing but you're as good as the owner already."

It hadn't been an easy decision, but the house by Lake Caroline was hands down the best option he'd seen. He'd given it a go, seen a bunch of "plantation" homes that, with a significant amount of elbow grease, could be mashed into something resembling Polina's dream. But after his dreaded conversation with the Boss, his money worries had practically vanished. Sokolov had a soft spot for his daughter and having her live in a substandard home in America was just not acceptable. Cal had convinced him that the home was as nice as any Antebellum home around, just without the huge plantation to go with it. He had explained to Sokolov's satisfaction that all the extra land, expense, and maintenance would only take away from his ability to be at Sokolov's beck and call, not to mention the unnecessary attention it would bring from the locals. This house was perfect and had a beautiful lake view from the upper balcony as well. Sokolov had reluctantly agreed to bump the budget up to over 600K but not without considerable grumbling and practically a whole fifth of vodka.

Now that Revolver was quickly consuming his life in just the three brief weeks since Adam had revealed the nature of his work, there was no way Cal could ever have overseen a plantation or huge home renovation project.

Besides, the idea of repairing a beat-up old house would, if anything, infuriate Polina more. She wasn't the type to be patient. Instant gratification was the way to go, and to be brought into a fixer-upper would surely push her "piss off" button. Better to use the Lake Caroline place as a launching point and float the idea of finding her actual dream home later.

She was still emailing him almost daily, and her letters had taken on a suspicious tone. Cal had refused to send her photos of the home over and over, and in time she began to suspect something was wrong. The previous day, after a particularly vague response, she'd called him in the middle of the night. It was more like that morning.

"What's wrong baby?" he'd asked, awoken from a dead sleep.

"I must speak to you about house," she'd said. Her voice had taken on an edge Cal wasn't familiar with. "You say you found a place, but you refuse to send picture. Why? What do you hide from me?"

"It's three in the morning."

"My papa says you are doing well at new job. That things are working well, and you have returned to your home in glory."

"I'm from Kentucky. Can we do this tomorrow?"

"I demand an answer, Cal. You cannot hide from me, not like this. Please, have enough respect to tell me if something is wrong."

Cal felt his heart soften as guilt crept in. Well, she did deserve an answer. After all, she'd have to live there as well. It wasn't just his house. He decided that if he was going to lie, he needed to at least soothe her in some way, let her know that they wouldn't be living in a shack.

"I want it to be a surprise, baby," he said. "I want the first time you see the house to be when you come to America."

Polina was silent for a moment. "Can you at least tell me what it's like?"

"It's lovely. It's nestled on a beautiful lake. You'll love it."

"What color is it?"

"Polina, I need you to realize that not every house is going to look like Tara from *Gone with the Wind*. Times have changed."

"I understand that. I just want nice Southern home. Please promise me you can give me that much."

"I promise, Polina," Cal said. At least that wasn't a lie. "Now please, let me get some rest."

She'd relented at last and left him to get a couple hours of fitful rest before going to sign the closing papers. Something in her voice haunted him even now, as he capped the pen and shook the real estate agent's hand. Did all men feel a sense of foreboding after buying their first house, or was he just an exceptionally unlucky guy?

He drove back to the Hilton. It had become almost like home, and Cal was grateful that Revolver at least had some semblance of class. He only went into the office three days a week, as he learned the ins and outs of their system. They all seemed reluctant to have anyone stay there for very long, as if the place could be raided at any time. The only five-day-a-week employee was Meryl, who had proven to be an entirely useless airhead. She couldn't keep notes to save her life, constantly forgot to tell people that important calls had come in from Russia and had taken up vaping. She'd blow huge white clouds that smelled and looked like cotton candy halfway across the office, only stopping when Cal yelled at her to put the android cigarette down. Whenever he went to the desk and asked her to make a copy of something, she would hastily close the window she was in, but Cal still recognized them as video games.

As for Adam, he had vanished. He didn't answer calls and never came into the office, preferring instead to issue commands in single-sentence emails from burner addresses. Cal was left to his own devices, struggling to untangle the complicated systems the Russians had set up stateside.

Much of it was devoted to phishing, stealing people's information via simple email queries. Some of it was outright hacking. Any delusions he could have allowed himself in Breznygrad about the questionable legality of his actions had vanished. Revolver was straight up digging through databases, most of them private, all of them at least tortuously related to either international shipping or local and state politics. Sokolov's enterprise was an espionage agency with a lumber side business.

Sometimes Cal wished that Adam had told him more. Laying as much down as he did when they spoke to the balding man had been surprisingly soothing. But much of the information he dealt with daily was still frustratingly cryptic, dropped off by men and women he'd never seen before with accents that belied their origins in other states and even regions of the country. It seemed that anything more important than a county sheriff's race was not entrusted to him, nor was it even transferred via Internet. Most of them wouldn't even speak to Cal, but one of them had shaken his hand, a gregarious older woman named Eva.

"I'm not supposed to do this," she said, winking. "But if you're ever in D.C., come by. We can talk shop. They don't look twice about our line of work out there." She pressed her business card into his hand. If she didn't look so much like a lesbian, he'd have thought she was hitting on him.

Cal unlocked the door to his room and lay on the bed. The feeling of triumph at closing the house still wouldn't come. He tried to think of Polina, but even she fell from his mind. All he could think about was the damn files.

He got up and walked to the phone, ordered a club sandwich and a beer to be brought up at once. He sat at his desk and opened the laptop Revolver had given him. Thirty-two gigs of RAM seemed a bit much since all files would be stored externally. He hooked up the external hard drive he'd been issued and pored over the files, stopping every time he saw the name ARMSTRONG. Who was he?

Cal would be flying back to Russia in a week. He'd get a connection at Dulles, with a long layover. When he went, he would have something to bring back. Just a terabyte single external hard drive this time, and from the filenames, most of it to do with Sokolov's shipping competitors. But still.

The way it worked was each file was password protected. Once Cal got back to Russia, he'd split them into individual flash drives. The contact, whoever they were, had the password, and only they could unlock the file. The drive itself logged each user, every attempt made to decrypt a document, every laptop it was plugged into. The drives themselves would pass through multiple hands, all of them loyal to Sokolov. Now that he had a Revolver machine, there was no chance Cal could get away with even plugging the drives into his personal computer, let alone copying the files. If he tried to decrypt them, it would be quicker and less painful to shoot himself in the head.

He made a mental note to stash his pistol at his new house before getting on the plane.

There was a knock on the door. A pretty girl handed him the tray with a smile.

"You've got a message," she said. "Right there next to your sandwich. It's from Adam."

"Adam?"

"We got eyes everywhere, Calvin Singer," she said.

Cal took the tray. His heart was in his throat. As soon as she was gone, he unlocked the safe and took out his pistol. Then he slowly opened the note.

Be careful what you believe, it said. *Eva loves to brag.*

Who could have known he'd been speaking to Eva? Cal swallowed deep. Maybe the place was bugged?

No, it was easier than that. Meryl.

Cal let out a string of curses. How could he be so foolish? Why else would she be there, if not to be a rat? He forced himself to be calm. Adam's note sounded more like a friendly warning than a threat. Meeting Eva was, therefore, a foregone conclusion. Did they want him to go? Was there more information in store, a necessary element to his training? Or was this a test?

He pulled Eva's card out of his wallet. The design was like Adam's, though she was only a vice president, and the company was called Patriot Solutions instead of Revolver. Looked like they didn't want to spend too much on design. Cal pulled out his cell phone and dialed her number. "Eva, Cal Singer here, what does your next Thursday look like, I've got a 2 and half hour layover in DC on my way back to Moscow, thought I might catch a cab and drop by for a few minutes."

"Sure thing, I plan to be here, please stop by"

✿ ✿ ✿

The Lake Caroline place was, in Cal's eyes, an absolute beauty. Five bedrooms, three and half baths, one bedroom that would make a very generous study, tile in the foyer, three-car garage, appliances so new the cling film was still stuck on the touchpad controls. The previous owners had been the first residents, and they'd stayed there less than a year before the husband died and the wife, wracked with grief, fled to her parents' home in Tampa. He could count on one hand the number of times he had been in a house this nice, none of them particularly pleasant. But now it was all his. Cal went from room to room and turned on all the ceiling fans and faucets in the toilets, listening with glee at the sound of all the taps running at once. In his childhood home the shower-head didn't work, and the tub faucet barely flowed, so they would have to fill buckets from the kitchen sink so they could take baths. Of course, Polina didn't need to know that.

Polina. She'd been on his mind constantly the past few days. He had been concerned, when he'd seen the place with half-packed boxes and battered furniture, that she would hate it, that it would be a disappointment. But now, cleared out and echoing softly, this house was the pinnacle of the American dream: clean, cozy, private. If she wanted to live like an American, there would be few places to better do it. The idea of the plantation house was ultimately foolish. This place, with the lake nearby and friendly neighbors, would be a far better location for them to build a life. She could still join the Junior League, invite her friends around for sweet tea and bourbon on the back porch. There was a boat slip in the back yard. *I can buy a nice boat for afternoon cruises. Polina would be in love with this place in no time,* he thought. This was nothing short of paradise.

He entered the garage. It was less thrilling for sure, being just a box with a concrete floor. Yet it was still a garage. The idea of Calvin Singer owning a garage would have been laughable up until this moment, and here he was pacing the length of it. It could use a good sweep, true, but nothing he couldn't wash off him-self. Along the right-hand wall near the door there was a series of cabinets built into the wall. Cal opened them. Roomy and in good shape. He felt along the back wall, then took this gun out of the holster and placed it in there, staring at it.

We got eyes everywhere, Calvin Singer. He hadn't been able to shake those words. How far did the reach of Sokolov's organization go? Was it only in the buildings and locations they placed him in, or was it elsewhere? How flexible were they, and how quickly could they find him? What would be considered a significant enough transgression for them to find him and put in work on his body? The image of Matt's pleading face back in Russia haunted him. Cal would wake up in the night, sweating, having stared at that face from behind his eyelids for hours, without relief. No judgment, and no words were spoken. Just that face, hanging there, haunting him, not in blame but in warning. It was as if someone was telling him, *this could happen to you.*

Guns. Cal needed weapons and armor to protect himself. On the off chance that shit went down, he wanted to be absolutely sure that he could take care of whatever it was, that he could fight his way through it and emerge the other side, not victorious, but alive. One pistol would not even come close to cutting it. No, he would need long guns, short-range engagement tools, firearms that could be easily concealed and big loud ones that could tear through Kevlar. He needed to get back in the gym, start training, be ready for whatever might come his way.

Cal picked up the pistol from where it sat in the cabinet and stood. In the case of an emergency, he sure as hell wouldn't be hunkering down in the garage or running out here to grab all his tools. He wandered through each of the rooms, analyzing them, considering the tactical advantages and disadvantages as best he could. He would need to make a more thorough investigation later, but for now he wanted to at least have an idea of what preparations would be made. Cal walked into the study, a.k.a. bedroom, and looked around. It was attractive, with nice paneling and good recessed lighting, an excellent place for a man to get some work done and retire to when the wife and kids were just a bit too much to handle. Calvin Singer with a study. His CO would shit himself raw if he saw this.

He spied a door he hadn't noticed the first time through. Cal opened it and let out a low whistle. It was a cavernous walk-in closet, long and narrow, with plenty of shelving. He walked to the end and ran a hand down the wall, as a vision came to him. Racks of weapons. Boxes of ammo. Yes, this would get the job done. He stashed the pistol atop the highest shelf along with two boxes of bullets. He'd be back for them shortly.

Seven

*T*he cab meandered through a kind of dumpy area of Washington, DC, mostly mixed-use and residential. He looked through the window of the cab, slightly disgusted at the urban decay but not overly worried or surprised. At this point, Cal knew what to expect from any kind of place Sokolov set up shop.

At least the plane ride from Mississippi had been good. Cal had sprung for first class, not on Sokolov's dime, of course. The Russian insisted on booking nothing but coach for his people, but Cal, sick and tired of the crappy leg room and terrible food, had bumped himself up. Yes, it cost, but it was a special occasion. After all, he was a homeowner at last.

As for the city itself, well. Cal didn't care much for DC. He had never been there before, not even in the military, and had only ever heard good things about it from the kind of boring pin-heads who loved America and watched the History Channel. For

Cal's money, it was a load of old shit, monuments that had darkened with age to overrated dead guys and pompous museums surrounded by dingy neighborhoods, tall buildings and stone, lots of stone. It boggled his mind to imagine people living there by choice. Anyone who made Washington their home would have to be invested in the apparatus of state and government, else, to Cal a least, there was no reason to make such a boring place home.

It made sense, of course, that Sokolov would have a presence here if his work involved lobbyists and other politicians.

The taxi pulled up outside a well-kept storefront that was nonetheless empty. Cal exited the cab and paid, leaving a modest tip. He stepped onto the sidewalk and looked up. Four stories, and old as hell but clean. More than could be said for some of Sokolov's other stomping grounds.

Being that it was a walk-up and not a proper office building, there was no counterpart to JD at this place. Cal buzzed the single button for the top floor and waited a moment. No answer. He buzzed again. Still no dice.

On the third try, the speaker crackled, and a harsh but somewhat familiar voice spoke out. "Yeah? What do you want?"

"Eva?" Cal said, hesitating. "It's Cal. From Revolver."

"Oh, hell. How are you?" Her voice changed immediately. "Come on up."

The door unlocked with an almighty groan, like a storm of mechanical bees. Cal shook his head and opened the door, mounting the obviously dated and worn linoleum stairs. When he hit the third floor, a door unlocked up top and Eva's head poked out.

"Hey there," she said. "Sorry about all that, I forgot you were coming into town."

"Oh, that's quite all right," Cal said, slightly winded. "I ain't too worked up about it. Think you got enough stairs in this place?"

Eva laughed. "Well, you know how the big man is. Hates to spend more than he must. This was the best we could get."

Cal finally arrived on the top floor, and Eva held out a hand in welcome. "How was your flight?"

He shook her head as warmly as he could, acutely aware of how damp his palms were. "Fine, quite all right I'd say. I'm coming in first class."

She let out a low whistle. "Fancy. Guess there's advantages to dating his daughter."

"This one is coming out of pocket. Y'all sure do love to gossip, don't you?"

Eva laughed. "Well, when you're running around six days a week it's good to decompress and vent. And besides, it's good to know what's going on in the other offices serving our mutual benefactor."

"Adam prefers to refer to him as 'the client.'"

Eva jerked her head a bit. "Adam likes to believe he's an equal to the leadership. And maybe one day he will be, but for now he's not a lot to look at. Me, I am fine where I'm at. Oh my, I shouldn't be saying things like that."

"No, you're fine. It feels good to be a bit more honest."

"Anyway, come on in. I'll show you the place."

The office of Patriot Solutions could not have been more different from the one at Revolver. Instead of a big open space, it was small and cozy with a surprisingly high ceiling, and only three very neat desks occupying the room alongside a full-size refrigerator with a microwave set atop it. While there were still two monitors on every desk, the place felt far less like a big, messy den for computer nerds to run tests. It was way too small to have a server room, too. There was also no one in there but Cal and Eva.

It made sense. Eva had a considerable different demeanor from Adam and Sokolov. Friendly and round, with her hair in a bun, and an attitude that was more suited for a Human Resources director than an operative for an organized crime syndicate that doubled as an unofficial espionage agency for the Russian government. Even her voice was a more cultured and upscale variation on the Midwest vernacular.

She waved her arms around the place. "You like it? Our boss over here isn't as much of a stickler as Adam, so we get something approaching an actual office. I kind of like it. Has a human touch."

"It's a lot cozier than Revolver, that's for sure," Cal said. "Where's your server room?"

She pointed down through the floor. "Basement, although we're a bit more tightly focused here. We are not doing anything more than we must out here on account of the feds always snooping around. As far as they know, we are providing tech solutions for lobbyists, nothing more. Which is accurate. Take a seat, would you?"

Cal nodded and sat at one of the desks, stretching his legs. Eva walked to the fridge and pulled out a bottle of white wine. She grabbed a couple of coffee mugs and returned to Cal, pouring each of them a generous amount.

"Bit early for it, wouldn't you say?" Cal asked.

She shrugged. "We're not busy, and I've got company. Not every day there's a new kid coming in from the Deep South."

Cal looked around. "Yeah, doesn't look like a whole lot is going down right now. Which is funny, because it looks like you run a tighter ship than Adam does."

Eva shook her head. "I'm not the boss around here. I know it says VP, but then again everyone here is a VP. Makes us sound more important when we're speaking to our actual clients."

"And who are they?"

Eva brought her wine to her mouth and drank. She wiped her lower lip with a handkerchief and crossed her legs. "Why don't you tell me what you know, and I'll fill you in on the rest. It'll save me from having to repeat myself."

Cal recognized the trick, and at this point he found it aggravating. "Don't you have a favorite cozy bar nearby that we can slip off to for some real afternoon refreshment?" He rolled his eyes around the room, following the perimeter of the ceiling. " I mean," he mouthed silently, *are we being watched or heard*, "I am parched from the long flight, and this wine really isn't doing the job."

Eva smiled with a wink, "Sure but it's not necessary, I have had this place combed and swept clean on more than one occasion, I can assure you we are safe to talk, besides you don't have that much time before your connecting flight. Grab a cold beer from the fridge or there is a bottle of Jameson under the sink, if you'd like, I keep a little something around just for my friends"

Cal retrieved the Jameson and put some ice in his mug, after he downed the wine. "I know that Revolver works with all kinds of lobbyists and such at the behest of our boss. Helps them out with state and local elections." Cal poured about three fingers of Jameson over the ice.

"Oh my." She drank more wine. "Well, you're not far off there. Although that's a bit of a narrow view of it."

"And what is that supposed to mean?"

"Do you think of all this as one operation?"

"Why, sure it is. We all report to the same place, don't we? We are always getting our orders from the same mouths. I don't see any reason not to think of it as all one thing, even if it is a bit messy."

Eva ran a finger along her cheek. "Have another drink," she said. "I don't know how much they'll mind me saying, but you'll see why I'm not concerned in a moment."

She took out a sheet of paper and a pen and began to draw. "So, we all know the big man is in Russia. He's got his whole business, lumber and hardware, moving all kinds of product all over Eastern Europe."

"And a bit in the U.S. as well."

"Right, he's got his operations out here. And incidentally, those operations are a lot more legitimate than you might believe. Customs is surprisingly uninterested in where the stuff comes from or how we made it, so long as it is legal to import. But the big man's got this whole other thing he carried over from the Soviet days. He was a top-tier operative back then, as I'm sure you've heard."

"He had to step back afterwards."

"Without the apparatus of the Party and the reorganization and abolition of KGB, GRU, and all that Warsaw Pact shit, the new Russia didn't have a lot of means to defend herself on the intelligence front. I was just a child back then, but from everything I've heard, it was rough in the Yeltsin years."

"Wait a second," Cal said. "You're Russian as well?"

She gave a wry smile and winked. "He likes his dual citizens; I'll say that much. So anyway, there's a change in leadership, and they start rebuilding the security and intelligence apparatus. Naturally, they want experienced leadership. Except all those old guys have gone private sector. They're making money hand over fist filling in for the fallen enterprises of the Soviet era. So how do you get them to come back? Well, you take a cue from the capitalists."

"You privatize all of it."

"By the time all this went down, the Communist dream was dead. The model society? The new world, with Russia at the helm? By the time they tore down the Berlin Wall, all that was gone. Guys like the big man had to adapt, but they still felt a sense of love for their motherland. And so, they set this whole thing up."

She drew another circle next to the one that said *Lumber* and labeled it *Intelligence*, then drew two beneath it and connected them with lines, labeling them *Russia* and *U.S.*

"I guessed a lot of this," Cal said, "and I haven't been able to connect it to what I'm supposed to be doing at all."

Eva nodded. "You ever get the sense that you're being blocked from knowing what's going on everywhere else?"

"All the time."

"Why do you think that is?"

"I imagined it was because they weren't too keen on anyone having too much of an idea of what's going on."

"That's part of it," Eva said, seemingly pleased to be sharing a secret. She began to draw all kinds of circles all over the paper, labeling them with seemingly random words and acronyms. She held it up and showed Cal. "The other part is, we work independently. It's a business, see. There's no KGB to pay us. Even if the FSB wanted to keep track of everyone, it couldn't. We had to split all this up into territory and field of specialty, then establish cells like these. Independent businesses, every one of them."

"So, Revolver ain't got nothing to do with you."

"We dabble. Share resources now and again. If the big man needs to call us up and bang heads, it turns ugly fast. So, we've kind of learned how to work together. We go to this little school near Breznygrad, get our 'education,' then come back here and set up shop. And don't think for a moment that you're the only American, either. We pay pretty well, especially for those who can't get real work in their field."

"Is there any risk involved with me talking to you?"

She laid the paper face down on the desk. "Whoever was listening to you back in Mississippi isn't the same as whoever is listening to you here."

This was both a relief and a new shot of fear for Cal.

"Different territory, different rules, methods, people," Eva continued. "If it feels at times that you're herding a bunch of headstrong, unconnected little groups each doing their own thing, you'd be dead on."

"Well, I know the South well enough. So, they put me in the right territory, I'd reckon."

Eva grinned a bit. "No offense, but what you are doing down there is a bit smaller scale."

"How do you figure that?"

She ran her finger around the rim of the coffee mug. "DC is the seat of the federal government. It's risky for us to get too involved out here, but it's also incredibly rewarding. And sometimes we can give some real change."

Cal felt his heart race. "What are you talking about?"

"Do you follow politics at all? You remember the 2008 presidential election, during the primaries?"

Truthfully, Cal didn't give a tinker's damn about politics. To him, it was all a circus, a waste of time. More American decadence, more undeserving people arguing about all sorts of things he didn't really care about at all. In fact, there was a good chance that if he had known that this job involved dealing with political rats, he would have thought twice about signing up. But here he was, with no other choice than to power through and make it all work.

"I was around," Cal said.

"It was a particularly nasty little election cycle. Nobody really liked Bush, only the most hardcore war hawks and a few religious types. So, everyone was trying to prove they were everything he had not been accused of being, that they were to be taken seriously. Nobody wanted another war, but everyone was still scared of the terrorists. Americans have always had a difficult time with war. Always wanting to paint themselves the victim, to make it an act of defense. The rest of the world, we ... I mean, they, see it as an inevitability."

"Did I mention I was in the Army?"

"Then you'll know all about it."

"They kicked me out for fighting."

"My condolences. In any case, the big man had his preferences among the contenders, as did some other top-level guys in the Russian inner circle. Elections can, of course, be nudged one way or another in Russia, quite openly. It's part of politics, you see. But the U.S. is not like that. It took a deft touch, one that could only be given by, perhaps, some bright-eyed young tech people who had just come to Washington with perfect accents and winning smiles. Who could, perhaps, move things one way or the other, on both sides of the aisle?"

Be careful what you believe, Adam had said. *Eva loves to brag.*

"Are you telling me a bunch of Russians rigged the election?"

"Oh no, but we moved the needle with varying levels of success. Perhaps it was a story about something someone said to his wife, or a photograph of someone in Muslim garb, delivered at the right time to his primary challenger. A hot mic here, an old publication there. I must admit, it did not go as well as we hoped, but the big man, our mutual benefactor, he has done well despite it.

And imagine, the nation's first black president. A shame he backed the wrong horse. I might be sitting in the White House having tea with the chief of staff right now."

"Well, if he was playing both sides…"

Eva shook her head. "The general election is a nut we haven't been able to crack. Maybe 2016."

Cal sat back in his chair. At a loss for words, he took another gulp of his Jameson on the rocks. This was his opposite number in a Russian mob organization—that part at least made it plausible.

"You'll have to forgive me, Eva," he said. "But I find all this just the slightest bit hard to believe."

"I knew you would," she said, nodding. "And that's why I'm going to give you something." She went over to a drawer and rummaged around.

She turned back around and handed him a flash drive. "If anyone asks, I didn't tell you this. But the trackers they have installed on the drives you all use can't really see what you do with the files, just if you copy them. You hide them in a flash drive image of something else, maybe a Linux distro or something like that, and you can make a copy. Just be careful what you do to the drive. The encryption will be a lot weaker."

"What's on here?"

"That's what was on a drive I took to Russia a while back. I made a copy of it for you special. See, I keep particularly juicy fragments around, just in case." Eva chuckled. "Never know when I'll need to go missing."

"Do you not have utter loyalty to your Russian employer?"

"Cal, I'm a mercenary. I am an errand girl, a bag man, same as you. Well, not the same as you, of course. My work is a bit more glamorous." She flipped her short hair.

"But you belong to Russia."

"I belong to whoever pays me, and so do you. We are not like Grigori. We are not like Adam. They served in the Russian Army; they believe, truly, that they can turn the Russian Federation back into the USSR. Oh, they may seem loyal to the current regime. Who wouldn't? But you must know, they yearn for the glory days."

"And you?"

She shrugged. "My grandpapa was killed under Khrushchev, and my favorite uncle rots in a prison near the Crimea. My mother was charged with felony shoplifting and now cannot vote in the so-called Land of the Free. I am like you, Calvin Singer. I am a patriot of the world."

❋ ❋ ❋

His connecting flight on to Moscow didn't take off for another hour. Plenty of time to hole up at the chain coffee shop at the airport, boot up his laptop, and shove the flash drive in. Cal purchased a large black coffee not smiling at the friendly barista; he had begun to feel the Jameson and knew he now needed to be thinking as clearly as he possibly could. Now was not the time for joviality. He parked himself in a corner, his back to the wall, and was careful to check for cameras. Last thing he needed was someone glimpsing over his shoulder at what was almost certainly sensitive, illegal material.

He popped the flash drive into the USB port on his personal machine. The plan was to look at whatever it was, make an encrypted copy, and destroy the flash drive before he got on the plane. It wasn't that he thought he'd be caught. Carrying two laptops onto a plane would not be considered cause for concern. After all, lots of respectable people like him were issued machines by their work, machines they would not use to Skype with their kids and work on their screenplays about a long-suffering insurance claims adjuster that would never see the light of day. But on the off chance they did try to investigate, it would be all too easy for them to look at this flash drive.

He opened the files inside. Sure enough, it was an image for an operating system. Cal moved it over to a virtual machine and mounted it, picking apart the files until he found something that did not belong. From there it was a matter of running a crack on it. Altogether, this wasn't much of a hiding job, but then again Eva had specifically mentioned that this wasn't meant to be well defended against prying eyes.

There were three files; one was a list of names that did him no good without context, another was a very boring collection of emails about Democratic National Convention voting practices. There were damning implications, if he read it right, but nothing that was, to the best of his knowledge, illegal. The last was a set of photos, labeled SEARS; he opened the file, saw what was there, and immediately shut the top of his laptop.

His first reaction was to throw the whole thing in the trash, but that was not possible. He felt infected, that the laptop was now cursed, and by extension so was he. Cal felt himself shake a bit, involuntarily. He wasn't sure he would ever be able to get the feeling out of him. The acts in that first image were too unsettling to consider. His mind wandered back over them, and he retched slightly even though he had barely eaten, covering his mouth. Cal had uploaded a facial recognition search engine and could easily see that the man in the photos was none other than George Sears, the junior senator from the state of Wisconsin. A junior senator who was not friendly to Russia, who used harsh language that called to mind the Cold War, who had, just weeks before, announced that he would not be seeking a second term. Cal had no knowledge of the senator or most any senator for that matter, but he felt he now knew plenty enough on this man for his liking.

Again, it wasn't clear if anything was illegal. They all looked well over eighteen. But it was the kind of material that if leaked would lead to an immediate resignation and total ostracization from polite society. Trembling, Cal opened the computer and looked through the rest. There were dozens of them, each worse than the last, and while most of it seemed consensual, not all of it did. They were all taken in a hotel suite. Many women, and a few men, not all of them conscious, and some of them bleeding. Out the window in one of the shots the skyline of Moscow could be clearly seen.

So, this was the plan, then; bring officials into the country, wine and dine them, then get compromising material and ship it back through a series of couriers. Real KGB shit, by Cal's estimation. He looked down at his bags and wondered what horrors could be held on the drive he was carting back, what had been shielded from his eyes.

On his screen he moved the files to his main drive, then renamed and locked them down as best he could. The text files may have been less lurid, but he felt certain they would be just as useful. When he got back to Mississippi, he would take a cue from Eva and make a copy. Stash a flash drive somewhere; hopefully in his new house, just in case this whole operation went belly-up. If the Russians could leverage this into damaging the career of a promising young senator, then Cal could surely do the same to help himself along.

He heard a reminder over the PA to check in for his flight. Cal pulled the drive and repacked his bag. In the bathroom he crushed the flash drive into as many pieces as he could with the heel of his shoe and flushed it down a toilet. He picked up his bags and made his way to the security checkpoint and on toward Russia.

Eight

*T*he ad was written in a tone of quiet desperation. *Brand-new house needs to go ASAP … Beautiful tile foyer … new appliances … $620,000 … come on down and see it RIGHT NOW!* The owner had sprung for a photo. The black-and-white image showed a decently sized brick-faced affair, the kind of place they had put up by the thousands across the Midwest and South during the housing boom.

He read it for about the fifth time out of the corner of his eye as he navigated the subdivision. This would be his first time seeing the house that he'd spotted in the Sunday paper. They had taken out a big *For Sale by Owner* ad in the classifieds. From the look of it, he had a feeling this owner had written it himself. He did not look forward to meeting this guy.

The house was on a quiet street in a subdivision wedged between Lake Caroline—a man-made, 850-acre fishing and recreational lake—and the well-designed golf course. They'd been developing and building this place up for about two decades now, taking it from dirt lots into a manicured and pleasant stretch of meandering streets lined with modest yet upscale houses. Harry was kind of torn when it came to subdivisions. On the one hand he appreciated the combination of a neighborhood feel with the intensely green, tightly planned luxury of a gated community. On the other, he kind of preferred the extremes of housing: the luxury high-rise and the sprawling rural home. He had had been a construction project and operations manager at a large firm before he joined the Company, specializing in commercial development.

Since retiring in 2008 from a thirty-six-year career as an executive in the construction trade, Harry had become bored and anxious with nothing to ply his years of skill to other than mowing his one-acre yard and edging the seemingly endless driveway. His home in the North Delta of Mississippi was in an area of primarily agriculture, entertainment was scarce as were fine dining establishments. Harry had begun to ponder what a new path of work he might like to get into; something fun and dynamic, one that might save him from becoming a couch potato like all his buddies that had gone before him. *I'm still young. I'm only 58, and I feel like I could go on for years and years.*

Harry had divorced many years earlier and thought it about time to move on and that a change of scenery might improve his mood. Afterall, he had practically married his job, thus many of his old friends had stopped calling or coming by. Harry was rarely home or when he was, he was either plotting his next big project or taking care of things around the house, never seeming to have time to socialize. He'd been gone so much that he had even lost his chair at the coffee shop where for over twenty years, he had joined his buddies every morning at six a.m. to shoot the breeze and hear the latest man-gossip. His children were all grown and had their own families now. His daughter still lived nearby, but his son, the older of the two, was living in Madison, Mississippi, had married and now had three young boys. The house was quiet, empty of a wife and children and seemed far too large for just him.

Harry decided that Madison was the place he wanted to retire. It was a progressive area with lots of entertainment venues and very good restaurants. He would buy a smaller home, he thought, hopefully on a good fishing lake not too far from town. He thought maybe he could get closer to his grandboys by teaching them to fish there. Harry's oldest son had offered his bonus bedroom above the garage for him to stay until he could sell his current home and find a new one close by. Harry moved in with little more than a suitcase, hanging bag, and his laptop.

Not long after settling in he enrolled himself into the local satellite campus of Tulane University in Madison. He'd opted for a degree in criminal justice with a minor in police studies. Harry had always had an affinity for doing sleuthy things, like undercover investigating and sneaking around. Years ago, he would stay awake into the wee hours of the morning watching Basil Rathbone as Sherlock Holmes and even today was hooked on watching every law and order movie or series on tv that he could stay awake long enough to watch. In his early years, he had even dressed up like a carpenter and pretended to be looking for work, applying at all the other companies in the area, just to learn what their prevailing wage was for his skill. It would help him in his cost estimating for bids on new work for the firm. He had played undercover boss with several of his own employees, not only to study efficiency but to understand their satisfaction with the firm, or lack of it.

He felt that going back to school might be a great use of his retirement time, since he had so much of it on his hands now and it would add a little flare to his life. Little did he know that he would attract the attention of the CIA. Unbeknownst to Harry, one of his instructors was close personal friends with the Deputy Operations Director in Washington who still retained a residence in Madison. They'd been college roommates back in the day and he had given him Harry's name as great employment candidate. Harry had excelled in his class work and was about to graduate in the top-five of his class.

As the graduation ceremony came to an end and the crowd was thinning out, a man not known to Harry approached him, as he was headed out to the front door. "Hello, I'm John Starke, Deputy Operation Director for the Central Intelligence Agency," as he stretched his hand out to shake. "You're Harry O'Keefe, is that right?"

"Yes, sir," Harry replied as he grabbed the man's hand, "What can I do for you, Mr. Starke?"

"I'm told that you are one of the top students of the graduating class, Mr. O'Keefe. I'd like to discuss the possibility of you applying to the Central Intelligence Agency as a contract employee, would you be interested?"

"Well, thank you, sir, what is that exactly? I never really expected to be re-employed, I just took this course to have something to fill my day with."

"Mr. O'Keefe, the CIA needs good men like yourself, especially those with a skillset such as yours, you were an executive for a large commercial contractor most of your working career, is that correct?"

"Yes, sir, but what would the CIA have need of a construction contractor for?"

"Tell you what, here is my card. My office is in Washington, my direct line is there as

is my email address; could we set up a time to discuss this next week over the phone? I am sure you'll be interested in the opportunities the CIA has to offer and the pay is pretty nice as well."

"Sure, when would you like to talk again?"

"I'll be back in my office next Thursday, could you call me around 2:00 p.m., your time?"

"Sure thing, thanks for reaching out, it's a pleasure to meet you."

Harry and John spoke the next week, and Harry agreed to submit all the forms and documents he requested. The long and short of it, Harry became an independent contract employee with a specialization in intelligence discovery and reporting. He would be charged with collecting and reporting on whatever mission he was given by his "handler" and while the rule was, all agents for the CIA were to reside in Washington DC, Harry was given a 36 month contract with no promise of extension, due to his already being at the top of the age requirement. He was to station himself in the Jackson, Mississippi metro area.

But this trip was not all about CIA business, Harry was in Madison for personal reasons, he was shopping for his new home. To Harry, no matter how far he went or what he saw out there, this stretch of Mississippi would always be home. Of course, things had changed over the years. Local government had been trying to bring in new industry for years, which meant new office parks, residential development, and an expanded service industry and even a Nissan auto manufacturing plant; it was a first for Mississippi. Nevertheless, the soul of the place had remained the same. It was still an honest, friendly place to live, picturesque and hot as hell in the summer. Harry thought of an adage used by true Mississippians, *"If you don't like the weather here today, stick around, it will be different tomorrow."*

Harry smoothly guided his pickup around the circle and pulled into the driveway of 109 Southampton Circle. He had to double-check it against the encrypted message from his handler one more time. He had a list of other real property to view on his on time but he'd been instructed to meet the owner of this home and learn as much about the property and the owner as he could, as if he were truly interested in purchasing the home. "Why am I looking at this house and this guy, what do I need to know about him?" he had asked his handler. She said "Its your first mission, that is your orders, you just follow through with what you can learn, make your report and we will take it from there. Details are not important to you at this time"

All these new subdivision houses looked the same to him. This one stood out, though, but not in a positive way. The house itself looked fine: brick façade, well-maintained and gently sloping roof, arced overhang at the front door to protect visitors from rain, newly color-stained and sealed driveway. It was the landscaping that really set it apart. Whoever lived here had apparently decided to really stretch their creative muscles with the garden. A raucous assortment of flowering bushes lined the entire front of the house, protected by a garden wall in a truly offensive shade of purplish gray. There were roses, mums, azaleas, petunias, a riot of color and leaves in various stages of blooming. Trellises were stuck seemingly at random, half of which were festooned with vines. A squat palm tree that had seen better days sat in the exact center of the front lawn, ringed around with nasty mulch and that same hideous stone. The overall effect was that of someone attempting to replicate elegance and failing horribly.

Harry got out of the truck and stared, taking it all in. He checked his notes again. There was no For Sale sign in the front yard, but he'd been instructed on what to tell the owner when he arrived at the house. There was no sign of the poor landscaping in the grainy black-and-white photo he had also been issued. It seemed this photo was taken before the garden was ruined.

He had to pick his way through potted ferns to get to the front door. Knocking as politely as he could. No answer. He knocked louder, and this time an answer came in the form of a loud, incoherent scream. It was a woman's voice, and the language was foreign. He knocked once more, just as the door was jerked open and a woman stood before him, wearing a full-length floral print sundress and a look of utter disdain. Her dark hair was cropped short and uneven, and she had the look of someone who could happily go their whole life without speaking to anyone ever again.

"Yes? What is it?" she asked. Her English was heavily accented, Russian from the sound of it. But there was also an odd, unpleasant twang, almost as if she was affecting a Southern drawl and failing miserably.

"Ah. Yes." For a moment he was taken back by her abruptness. "I'm here to see the house?"

The woman's demeanor softened, but not by much. "Cal!" she shouted over her shoulder. "Someone here to see the house."

A man's voice shouted back unintelligibly, but apparently that was enough for the woman.

"You can come in," she said. She looked down at Harry's worn but well-kept leather shoes. Not exceptionally tidy, but far from dirty. "Take off shoes. Or put on boot cover." She waved toward a small box of cloth booties.

"Sure, thank you," Harry said with a smile, stepping into the small, tiled foyer.

The woman grunted and walked away, leaving him to struggle as he slipped the cloth booties over his own shoes. It took some doing but he finally got them all the way on. He straightened up and took his first look around the place.

His first impression was that he had entered a thrift store that specialized in items too tasteless to be accepted elsewhere. There were no less than three ornately carved side tables that he could see from his narrow vantage point in the foyer, and a large watercolor landscape in a gaudy frame hung against the wall to his left. Harry wasn't sure what he had expected, but it was not this.

Suddenly a tall, young, lanky guy with a shock of sandy hair came bounding into view. The man stretched out his hand and took Harry's, engaging him in an enthusiastic handshake.

"Cal Singer. Pleasure to meet you," the homeowner said. He continued to pump Harry's arm like he was trying to get water. "You've met the wife already?"

"Why, yes," finally extracting his hand from Cal's grip. "She was very gracious. My name is Harry O'Keefe. Nice place you have here. Good friend of mine, a Realtor named John Malouf, he called you about my looking at the place?"

"Sounds about right."

"Well, he's been keeping an eye out for me for quite a while and says your home is what I've been looking for. Looks great, from what I can see so far." Harry would never tell Cal what he really thought of the furnishings, and certainly not at this point in their relationship.

Cal laughed humorlessly and tapped his nose. "You don't have to lie to me, Polina can be a real handful. Met her in Russia and married her a year later, biggest mistake of my life. Kidding, of course, all jokes. We have fun around here. Good Lord, she's got you wearing the booties. That woman is absolutely obsessed with her carpets and hardwood floors. Well, come on in, then. I suppose you didn't come here to listen to me jaw on and on for hours."

Harry nodded and followed Cal into the living room. Cal was not what he expected either. The guy could not have been over thirty-five, but he had both the weary pretention and worn looks of a much older man. On top of that, there was something artificial in his joviality. His raw, lean physique implied not cordial hospitality but barely contained violence. Harry wondered if the violence was controlled or exasperated by Polina's hostility.

"All right then," Cal said. He swept an arm around him. "So, this here is the living room. Or the parlor, as my wife says."

The junk store effect was even more pronounced here. There were so many antique buffets and china cabinets, hideously uphol-stered sofas, and tasseled ottomans that it was hard to move around.

The only presentable part of the room was the immaculately clean white carpets.

"You got quite a collection in here, Mr. Singer."

"Cal, if you please. Can't bear my family name. You can thank the wife for all this fancy junk. She's got quite the appetite for ugly ornate shit." He leaned toward Harry conspiratorially. "If you want to purchase any of it, I'd be only too happy to oblige. The less of this trash moves with us, the better."

"Where are y'all moving to?"

Cal threw his hands up. "That's the best part. I have absolutely no idea. The wife has had it in her mind to live like a Southern belle. Wants us to have a daughter so she can go to the cotillion or whatever. So now we need to find a plantation house for her to live in. And her PAPA, well, he just won't have his baby girl unhappy."

Harry nodded. "You know how fathers can be. They're always wanting what's best, even when it isn't feasible."

"My father wasn't much to look at and didn't think much of taking care of us. And honestly, I would not even care what her daddy wants. I believe a man should be the head of his house, not tossed around. But the guy signs my checks, so what can you do. You want to see the rest of the place?"

"What is it you do, Cal, if I may ask? And yes, absolutely. I would like to see it all. That's exactly why I'm here, I'm seriously looking to buy and the sooner the better."

Cal smiled, but his eyes stayed glassy. "Bit of this and that. Enough about me. This here is the dining room. Not much to look at either—you can see even more of her crap. This table cost two month's mortgage, so that one isn't for sale. I guess I should have asked earlier, but what are you in the market for, Harry?"

"I honestly really like the wallpaper," Harry said. "Well, I've been in building and land development for years, mostly operations and such. My old employer had me all over the country for years, which I really enjoyed, but in time that running and gunning kind of wore me down. I just switched firms, and I'm looking for a nice place on the water. Not much yard but maybe a boat slip? Something for me to settle down in, take grandkids fishing too, you know."

"We've never eaten so much as a biscuit in this room. We always eat in the kitchen. Come on, let's look at the kitchen. A new job?" The veneer of Cal's politeness cracked a bit. "Aren't you a bit old to be bouncing around like that?"

"I'm afraid there wasn't much of a choice. You know how it is nowadays. Economy is in a slump; things are not what they used to be. When I was your age, I wasn't expecting to be switching around. Had a great employer, a great firm that was growing like a weed. But there you have it. Besides, I won't be moving around so much from here on. I'll be sixty soon, I got a pretty nice nest egg, and I'll be able to retire in a few years. Would like to just be able to wet a hook, play some golf, and watch the lake from my back porch with a cool cocktail in the afternoon."

"This is the perfect place for that. You also got The Mermaid just around the corner. Great steaks and some of the best fish around here. When you go, tell Brian at the bar I sent you. Polina hates it, which makes it an excellent place to hide." He winked conspiratorially. "Here's the kitchen."

The kitchen, at least, seemed normal. There's only so much that can be done to a kitchen, and while Polina had hung some rather garish paintings of dogs and relocated some of the outside vegetation to a vase on the island, for the most part this at least matched the description on the ad. Harry looked around with a faint smile. He hated the ceramic countertops and black appliances but didn't mention it. He could always fix that up with some new granite tops and a quick trip to Cowboy Maloney's over in Jackson.

Cal opened the fridge. "She don't cook much anymore, but she had us remodel the kitchen anyway. So, these appliances are basically brand new."

Harry peered inside. You can tell a lot about someone from the inside of their refrigerator. Cal and Polina's was almost empty, save for a few open wine bottles, takeout containers, and about twelve different kinds of mustard. *What kind of person keeps red wine in the fridge?* he thought.

"Good to know," he said.

Cal grunted and slammed the door. "The garage is out the side door. One of the two places in here I spend my time." He led Harry down a narrow hallway past what appeared to be a home office–styled room, the door only partially open. When he peeked in, he could see military-style stuff lying on the floor and stacked against the wall, but with the door almost shut he could only see just so far. There was what looked like a flak jacket, as well as a helmet. He thought it best if he didn't ask.

There were two cars in the three-car garage: a newish orange-gold Hummer and an aging Cadillac. The other full third of it was taken up by workbenches and a vast assortment of odds and ends, all stacked up against the wall under the window.

"Mind if I take a closer look?" he asked Cal.

"No please, take as long as you need. I am anxious as hell to get this place gone. I have had nothing but hell since I moved us in here. Sorry we're flying through it like this."

"What's the big hurry to get out of here? This is a great neighborhood from what I'm told, is there something I need to know? I mean is the foundation okay? Termites? Or are the utilities and taxes a rip?"

"Oh no," Cal responded. "This is a great place, I love it, and the taxes are not so bad. I'm just a bit homesick for Kentucky, and the wife is miserable here. She's always wanted something bigger and better; you know how they are, the grass is always greener, right?"

A stack of boxes sat precariously next to what looked like a whole trampoline broken into component parts. Harry tried to peer in and around them, to no avail.

"Can I take a look at the wall?" he asked. "Just trying to be thorough, no mold or foundation settlement, you know." What was it the Company wanted me to find, secrete panels, trap doors, what was it, Harry wondered?

"Well, I suppose so. You need to be very careful; all that shit is just stacked on top of each other, and it ain't real stable. I can be kind of a pack rat, but I guess moving might let me get rid of some of this stuff."

Harry moved the stack, an inch at a time, until he glimpsed the wall. Wasn't anything to see back there, just a normal wall painted light taupe. It was mildly disappointing, but he decided to improvise. He stacked the boxes back. Surely there was a hidden compartment somewhere in this house, somewhere out of site to the average person, where is it, Harry wondered.

"Watch out there," Cal said. "You don't want that whole thing falling over."

Harry made a noise of assent and slid them back being careful to lean them up against the trampoline frame. He figured it wouldn't take more than quick jerk for the whole load to fall over.

"Well, it's a wall," he said.

"Not sure what else it could have been."

"You said this is where you spend about half your time? You mind if we look at where you spend the other half of your time? Can't hurt to know where to hide from the old ball and chain." Harry couldn't shake the image of the military gear from his mind.

Cal grinned and waved him back in the house.

❀ ❀ ❀

The rest of the tour was largely truncated. Cal ran Harry through the master bedroom and spare bathroom, both of which Harry claimed he was woefully unequipped to assess. He said, "I'll need to bring my lady friend over later, since she is the one who is far more particular about such things." This was only partially a fabrication: Harry wasn't immune to the charms of a nice bathroom by any means, but for him, so long as the commode worked, it at least had a shower and wasn't overly drafty, any bathroom got the job done.

So that's how they came to the last of the five bedrooms, which Cal threw the already partially cracked door open with a flourish.

"It took me a long time to win this one," he said with pride. "We get a place with five bedrooms, and we don't have a single kid between us. I'm thinking she is waiting until we get to her dream house. So, I convince her to let me turn the bedroom I like best into a study, and boy, did I run with it. Had to let her purchase that awful safari-looking piece of shit we sleep on, but it was worth it."

Having known Cal for about an hour, Harry wasn't sure what to make of him. The guy was odd and jittery. He seemed like the kind of guy who worked himself into a lather so often that he couldn't gain weight and instead just wasted away, tightening like beef jerky under the sun. On top of that, the way he talked about his wife was off-putting. Now Harry's orders were not to get too personal with his questions, least he roused suspension but the whole thing looked like a real mail-order bride situation to him. Their barely contained dislike of each other kind of seeped into every corner, was expressed in every awful decorative choice. Part of Harry worried that being here too long would poison him to a future full-time partner, turn him into a bitter, dried-up husk like the current homeowners. Harry had a job to do so he had to focus of the mission.

But he had to admit, it was a nice study.

They had built bookshelves into the walls, although there were more University of Kentucky sports memorabilia than books. There was some accent paneling, and the walls were painted a rich clubhouse green. The desk was expansive and had a top-of-the line office chair behind it. There was plenty of seating for guests as well and a flat-screen television bolted into the wall.

"If I didn't know better," Harry said, "I'd think you'd built yourself a man cave in here."

"That's what Polina said," Cal laughed. "I insisted that every single piece of this place was needed for me to do my job. That's the one thing she don't mess with. I tell her it's for work, she clams right up, doesn't want to hear it. Apparently, her daddy brought it home with him, and she don't want to live like that. I don't believe it. Here's the good part."

Cal walked over to a door and opened it up to reveal a walk-in closet. The shelves were stacked with cigar boxes, knife cases, several bottles of dark liquor, a few high price bottle of Vodka, and at the far end, a vintage rifle. He led Harry back and removed the rifle from the wall.

"Mosin-Nagant. Got it from one of her daddy's friends for an absolute steal." He cradled the Russian firearm like a child. "In great shape, too. Old as hell, but it still shoots straight. You like shooting, Harry?"

"Now and again. What good Southern boy doesn't?"

Cal laughed. "You're right there. Anyway." He hung the rifle up. "Oh, and this back wall comes down too. I'd open it up but I'm afraid what's in there's private." He winked. "I'll be honest, it's mostly girlie mags. Collected a lot of them over the years. Not much else to do when you're in the military. Anyway. Stay for a drink, and we'll get to know each other."

He grabbed a bottle off the shelf seemingly at random along with two glasses and sat on his desk. Harry took a seat in an overstuffed leather chair and crossed his legs. Cal poured two fingers of scotch into each of their glasses and handed one to Harry.

"Thanks," Harry said. He clinked glasses with Cal and brought his to his mouth, barely wetting his lips. He hated scotch but would pretend to like it for this conversation.

Harry couldn't help but look at the military hardware laying around and a couple more long-guns in the corner. "You in the military reserves or something."

"Nah, not anymore, I just like collecting that sort of stuff, you know like the rifle I just showed you. I go out with some locals from time to time shoot targets and drink a little beer, that all."

Cal began, as if to get away from the gun subject as quickly as he could. "All right, so… I'm guessing you're from around here?"

"Clarksdale, born and raised. Cotton fields and the home of the blues, lots of dust and grit. Got real deep roots there, but I have friends and family spread out all over Mississippi. Hell of a good place to live."

"I hear that," Cal said. "I came up in coal country. Owensboro, Kentucky."

"That explains all the University of Kentucky stuff."

"Big fan, despite myself. Some things run deeper than I would ever like to admit. Still, I don't got a lot of love for the place. Everything looked like shit, and the people were meaner than hell."

"You get that far north people start to lose their manners."

"You're damn right they do."

"I heard you say something about being in the military."

Cal swigged half his liquor. "You consider yourself a patriot, Mr. O'Keefe? I'd hate to offend you."

"I like to think I am, Cal. My Dad was a Marine, fought in Iwo Jima during WWII, he was a great guy, tough a hell Dad, but looking back, I'm glad it was his way or the highway. That's what made me the kind of man I am today."

"Well, I am too. But when it comes down to it, I don't think much of the military anymore. I was in the Army for a few years. Saw a little action. I set up all our infrastructure over in Iraq like it was nothing. Built the whole server farm from scratch. Boy, was I proud of what I was doing. You might not believe this, but I ain't never been much. Mostly just a dirt-poor son of a mean-ass career military man, hated me because I couldn't fit the bill of a military academy stiff. I ended up joining the regular Army just to stay out of trouble. After a while I started fitting in, felt like I was finally part of something good. Till I wasn't, of course."

"Sounds like you're a bit of a patriot yourself," Harry said.

"I guess so. In my own way. Anyway, after I got my discharge I came back stateside, and you know what? Nobody was willing to give me a job. No sir, they all said I was either too qualified or not worth a damn. So, I flunked around the whole lower forty-eight until I found myself here. And I knew if I could just get a little money together, I would be content to make this place home. But that didn't work either."

"So, how'd you meet Polina then?"

"Went over to Russia on the advice from some local computer geeks I'd met. Applied my considerable skills in cybersecurity to her father, who by the way, is loaded as hell. He is this wealthy industrialist, basically runs the lumber business over there. He's a real old-school guy—you'd like him. Not like these phony Silicon Valley types in their hoodies and tennis shoes." Cal poured himself another drink.

"I hope you stay in Mississippi," Harry said, pretending to take another sip.

Something like a shadow pulled at Cal's face. "Well maybe, we'll see. How about you? How's construction treating you?"

"It's a fine way to earn a living. Takes me all over the country. I've gotten to see some sights and have fun, but I'm hoping to settle down and kick back a bit. Kind of like you."

"Hell, I hope not. I'm stuck here. Don't get me wrong, I love it, but there ain't no way her daddy is letting me go. Needs me too bad over here."

"So, you work for a Russian company?"

Cal nodded. "One of his subsidiaries has an office here. Lumber, but also fasteners, sheet metal, that sort of thing. Place wouldn't run without me." The shadow pulled at Cal's face again, darkening his features, making him look suspicious. "I gotta ask, Harry. How come—"

Suddenly an almighty crash sounded from the direction of the garage, accompanied by a fresh round of screaming from Polina. Cal let out a string of curses and slammed his glass down.

"Now what?"

"Do you need any help?" Harry asked. He made as if to leave his chair.

"No, I'll take care of it. You just relax."

Cal left the room, slamming the door behind him. As soon as
the door hit home, Harry leapt to his feet. He didn't need to follow
to know what the noise was. It had taken longer for the cacophony
to go off than he had planned, but the precarious stack of boxes
must have fallen over and taken the trampoline with them.

He figured he would have the run of the house for a moment or
two. What he hadn't banked on was Cal just leaving him in the one
room he would want to look in. He could not believe how lucky he
was and almost suspected a trap. Harry opened the closet and crept
to the back wall, taking down the rifle. He slipped a finger along
the almost imperceptible gap and pulled the whole thing down.

Harry whistled softly. Well, it sure wasn't pornography Cal
was hiding. Instead he found a staggering array of loosely stacked
weapons. Just from a quick glance he could discern at least six
rifles, two shotguns, pistols hanging from the walls of the cubby, a
grenade launcher, and rounds to go with all of them. The guy was
hoarding weapons like it was about to turn into war zone any day
now. Even for an aficionado of weapons or someone concerned
about home defense, this was a bit much. Cal had an entire armory
back here in an insulated fake closet, hidden from everyone, his
wife included.

This was the work of a paranoid mind. Only question was, why
was he so afraid? And why would his handler not clue him in on
what was cooking with this guy.

He heard the garage door slam and more screams from Polina.
Cal yelled back. Harry quickly put the fake wall back up and hung
the rifle where it belonged before dashing back to his chair, making
it into the seat just before Cal swung the door open.

"Real sorry about that," he said. Whatever pretense of decorum he'd put on was shattered. "Bit of a spill, but of course that's too much for my wife. You know how women are."

"I'm afraid I don't. Me and mine get along very well, course we aren't married though."

"Hey that's great. Good for you." A scowl had taken up residence on Cal's face, and with it an air of barely cooled rage. "Listen, you better come back another time. We can work out the details later. I can't do business with her hollering."

"Well, don't worry about it too much, I'll take it."

Incredulous delight softened Cal's face. "You don't say. What's your offer?"

"The ad says $620,000. As such, I was thinking, $590,000."

"Why hell yeah, I'll take that, let's do this thing. Sorry, please excuse my Russian."

Harry allowed himself a smile. "It's all right. I know this is a good day for you. But I'll be honest, I have fallen in love with the place and I want it. Don't want anybody coming in and swooping it up." He offered his hand.

Cal grabbed it and started pumping again. "Guess I better find her a mansion quick! I cannot tell you how happy you're making me. It was the study what clinched it, wasn't it?"

"It didn't hurt, I'll tell you that."

"I knew it. You want it, it's all yours. We'll draw up some paperwork, and you can come back over and sign it."

Nine

C al found himself, the week after the handshake deal with Harry, sitting in his father-in-law's office in Breznygrad.

"Sir," he began, "have I got just the best news for you."

Ever since the untimely "disappearance" of Matt, it had fallen to Cal to get the drives back and forth between Russia and the U.S. At first, it was something he excelled at. His smooth, artificial charm was far more effective than Matt's brusque Jersey demeanor, and it played a lot better with customs agents and security forces on both sides of the Atlantic. And if ever there was a conflict of some kind, an issue wherein uncomfortable questions were asked or Cal was chosen for a random search, a quick smile and a phone call to Sokolov was all it took to handle the matter.

But the specter of Matt still hung over his every dealing. There was no denying that Matt was no longer among the living, even if the topic was never broached in the slightest. It was as if Matt had never existed, had simply been an error in an official report to be scrubbed out and replaced with another, more fitting American. Nevertheless, the knowledge that he was Matt's replacement never left Cal. Neither did his conviction, his firmly held belief, that if ever he were to cross Sokolov past the point of tolerance he too would be erased and replaced with another American, one even more pleasant and amenable, and even easier to control.

The whole business with the house had been a sore point. Sokolov had sent him to the States with the explicit mission to find his daughter a dream home, the plantation mansion of her dreams. Unfortunately, he also burdened Cal with an unreasonably small budget and a demand that he reside near Jackson, as the bulk of his work would be done, by a strange twist of fate, out of the very same building where he'd once worked as a security guard. The sum of these impositions left Cal with precious few options, and, unwilling to purchase some vast fixer-upper in the woods somewhere, he'd settled on the Lake Caroline place.

He knew it would not be what Polina wanted, and since at that point he was very eager to keep her happy, he found himself mildly dreading her disappointed reaction. But nothing could have prepared him for the storm of rage she unleashed upon him when she first saw the house.

She'd chattered all the way to the house from the airport, unperturbed by her husband's terse silence. Her own words had started to fade as he guided the car through the subdivision.

"Are we on our way to the farm?" She'd asked.

Cal had given only a grunt in response. His heart tightened and sank. Polina had fallen silent as he pulled into the driveway.

"Well," he'd said. "This is it. Should I carry you over the threshold?"

She'd been in the mood for no such thing. Instead her stony reserve continued as she followed him through the front door and into the empty foyer. Polina looked around her, slowly, seemingly in shock, before finally turning on her husband.

"When we married, you promised me beautiful plantation house," she begun. "You promised me verandas. Willow trees. *Gone with the Wind.*"

"Now, look baby," Cal had begun. She cut him off with a scream. Her first scream of many.

"But instead you bring me to this hovel! This is cabin. This is dung heap. You drag me away from Papa, from only home I've ever known, and you bring me here, to this?" She began to cry.

Cal had wanted to point out how much she hated her father's home in Breznygrad, how she had often called Paris a second home. He'd found her tears theatric, and some of his shame turned to anger. Still, he made as if to console her, and put his hand on her arm. But Polina had batted it away and began screaming again, threatening to divorce him on the spot, to call her father and have him fired. It had taken hours and much soothing, as well as a very expensive dinner at The Mermaid, to convince her that the house would do nicely, at least for now. He promised her that the mansion was coming, he just needed to get himself settled first.

The first couple of weeks had been an exercise in terror. Sokolov had given Cal a phone call, made him understand through barely contained rage that Polina's happiness was to be his singular priority, and that he had failed magnificently at finding her acceptable lodgings. They were to spend no more than two years in that house before finding a new one. Sokolov would alter Cal's salary appropriately, under the condition that he redouble his efforts. Suddenly the dynamic under which he had risen back to something like respectability had irrevocably shifted. Cal was now, through the demands of his wife, deeply in debt to Sokolov.

As for Polina, she had eventually settled into a resentful acceptance of her new life. She seemed to think of the Lake Caroline place as a kind of trial run for her inevitable rise to Southern belle. She festooned the house in heavy draperies, bought and sold various pieces of garish, ornate furniture, packed side tables with framed photos of wildlands she had never laid eyes on. She experimented with traditional down-home cooking, producing biscuits hard as rocks, burnt fried chicken, and greens so overcooked and unseasoned as to be inedible, all of it placed before a husband too frightened and stressed to give any kind of feedback. Her perception of the South was cartoonish, a comical and outsized notion borne of textbooks and films of a smattering of eras and locales that had nothing to do with contemporary Mississippi. It would have been offensive had it not been so inept.

That's why selling the house for sticker price, which was a full 100,000 dollars over his original purchase cost put Cal in such a good mood. Based upon his preliminary research, he would have enough for a down payment on a plantation-style home. Not necessarily historical or brand new, but one old enough and in good enough shape to satisfy Polina's insatiable desires for her off-brand Southern living. And in the process, he could return to his boss's good graces, where the chances of disappearance were considerably less.

Maybe he could find a nice place in Flora, it was only a few miles down the road, or just outside the square in Canton, at least there the town square had a lot of old South architecture or possibly near Vicksburg where there were many post-civil war homes but the drive to the office would be a bit longer. Cal knew he would just have to do a better job of searching for it this time, especially now that money was not an issue. His pay had increased exponentially since the purchase of the Lake Caroline place.

So that's why Cal smiled as he sat back in his chair in the cramped little back-room office with Sokolov, even though Volgin, the nearly-silent driver, loomed over him from what seemed like a great height.

"Yes, sir," he said. "You're really going to love this one."

"Well, out with it," Sokolov said. In the time that Cal had known him he'd become considerably less affable. The ongoing house debacle hadn't done anything for his mood.

Cal's smile faltered. "I've sold the house. We are on our way to Polina's dream home. Before long she'll be putting up pickled okra and having tea with the neighbors. Or whatever it is she's looking for."

Sokolov's face lightened ever so slightly. "Yes, this is good news. Brings me great joy to know darling girl will be living the way she should have been whole time." It was impossible to discern if this was sarcasm. "Where is the new house?"

"The new house?"

"Yes. The mansion I sent you there to find in the first place. What is it like? Tell me every detail. Show me photos."

Cal swallowed the stone of fear that appeared in his throat. "I'm afraid we don't have another house yet."

Sokolov stared at him for a moment. When he spoke, his voice was deadly quiet. "Then where will you live in meantime?"

"Well, we could stay in a hotel for a while."

Volgin laid a hand on Cal's shoulder, but as a comfort or a threat, it was impossible to tell.

"Hotel, you will put my daughter in a hotel?" Sokolov finally stood, and when he spoke, it reminded Cal of Polina's screams in the worst way. "My daughter will not sleep in hotel! It has taken two years for you to fail at task that should have taken two weeks. How difficult is it to purchase a house?"

"Actually sir, it's quite—"

"Shut up. I am not finished. Polina Popov should already have her home and fine carpet. She should be filling house with children and inviting ladies over, so they can become envious of her wealth. I pay you enough, I have given you enough. You have failed, Calvin Singer."

"I'm terribly sorry, I promise, it's been outside of my control. The housing market isn't what it used to be, and it's not exactly easy to find antebellum plantation homes around Jackson."

Volgin's grip tightened.

"Is this my problem? I do not think this is my problem at all. I think this is your problem, and you are too lazy to fix. That is what I think. And I think that maybe I should look at your other work. Maybe you are lazy there too? Finding house is so simple monkey could do it. Perhaps you are not so good with my computer?"

"I promise, Mr. Sokolov, my work for you is of the absolute finest quality. I swear it on my life. I will find Polina a house just as soon as I get back, and it'll be the best damn house in all of Mississippi. You have my absolute word on it."

"Your word is worth shit, Calvin Singer. Remember who signs your checks. Remember where I found you and remember where you will go if you do not perform as expected."

Cal swallowed deeply. He nodded. Volgin finally removed his hand.

"You'll be going to Atlanta next week." Sokolov returned to his seat, his face red and gleaming with moisture. "You will meet up with Adam again, do exactly as he says. Do not ask questions; prove you are worthy of my daughter."

❖ ❖ ❖

The trip back to Lake Caroline seemed to last forever. Cal made it through customs with little incident, but every moment was weighed down with intensified pressure. He'd thought that breaking the news to Sokolov would alleviate some of the strain, buy him enough goodwill to get everything sorted and the next, hopefully permanent phase of his life moving. But instead, the strain was doubled. There was a timer counting down to his possible death, and Cal had no idea how much time was left on it. His only hope at stopping it was to keep Polina happy. Surely his father-in-law did not want to see his daughter cry.

The honeymoon period between Cal and Polina effectively came to an end that first night they spent in the house. They did not make love that night, nor for many afterward, and whatever affection remained in Polina's heart for her husband seemed to drip out over the next few weeks. Their dynamic settled into tense silence punctuated by brief, loud arguments. Resentment had taken the place of companionship on both sides. Polina was eternally angry with Cal for breaking his promise of a beautiful Southern mansion, while he was frustrated with what he saw as a lack of compassion on her part. The fact that Sokolov and his influence over both of their lives hung over their every interaction only made it worse.

It seemed that a great deal rested on this Atlanta trip going well. Cal was already used to traveling around the South, mostly to uninteresting small towns. It seemed that whatever Sokolov's specific interests were in the U.S., he had divided the country into territories. Sometimes Cal would run into his West Coast or New York counterpart while in Russia. They would exchange a terse nod of the head and go about their business.

But this was the first time Cal would be going to Atlanta. Part of him was looking forward to the trip: he had not been to Atlanta in years, and more importantly, he'd get some time away from Polina and her family. He would be able to have a night alone, stay in a decent hotel, maybe go to a strip club. It would be an odd combination of vital business trip and welcome vacation.

He pulled the car into the garage and closed the door. Ever since Harry came around and the boxes tumbled in an avalanche, the place had been in a bit of disrepair. Regrettably, Cal had a bunch of sensitive items stashed, and the whole situation was a bit unsecure. He made a mental note to get the place in order before Harry came back to take another look.

Cal found Polina where he usually did when he came home: sitting in her giant recliner in front of the flat-screen television, watching a Russian soap opera on their extended cable package. He paid through the nose for it but thought it would be better not to complain.

He tapped her on the shoulder and smiled. "I'm home, dear."

She grunted. "Welcome back."

He sat down on the sofa caddy-cornered to her. "Your Papa is doing well. He's excited about the house selling."

"But we don't have another house yet," she said. Selling the place had not improved her mood as much as Cal had hoped.

"But we will soon. I promise, honeybun."

"You have nice words, but no action. What use are words? I cannot live in words."

Anger flared within Cal. He knew she was right but was loathed to admit it to himself. All her words did was remind him of all the people who would tell him, all through his life, that he could not talk his way out of everything. That sooner or later, he would have to take responsibility. But he never did. And now, confronted with a broken promise, his instinct was to fight back.

"You ought to be grateful, you know," he said. "I brought you out of that Russian shithole to the greatest country in the world. A man could use a little gratitude you know, instead of endless bitching and moaning."

"I am not a bitch," she said, voice rising.

Cal wanted to disagree with her but chose a different tack. "I'm not saying you are. I am saying I'm sick of hearing you complain. It's all I hear day in day out. Endless ungrateful complaining."

"You made me a promise. You did not keep it. And you are not even here to console me. You are always out of town, and if not then you spend all your time at Mermaid, or in study."

"Because I can't stand the sound of your voice."

"How dare you. Maybe I should divorce you. Would you like that? Would you like to explain to my papa that his youngest daughter divorced you?"

Cal fell silent. He could feel the heat in his face. He finally understood why men could beat their wives. His readiness for violence had always stopped at women, but this one didn't seem to understand how close he was to the edge. What she did seem to understand, implicitly, was that she held his life in her hands. Yet she didn't make many overt attempts to manipulate him with this information. Instead she just used it to end arguments. When she was tired of yelling or found Cal's tongue to be sharp, she would simply threaten to divorce him or complain to her father, and Cal would just shut up. It was as if she valued silence overall, which was remarkable considering the volume of her voice and how loud she would turn up the TV.

If anything, getting physical with Polina was a death sentence. So instead Cal just sighed and sank back deeper into the fake brocade couch. Whatever kind of place they moved into; he would have to be sure that there was a very large, very private study.

"Well," he said. "I'll be on the road soon. So, you won't have to deal with me."

"Where are you going?" Polina said with feigned interest.

"Atlanta."

Her false curiosity turned to genuine enthusiasm. "I have always wanted to go back to Atlanta."

"Really? No kidding. I guess everyone does."

"You must take me with you."

Cal's heart sank. "It'll be boring, dear. It's just a two-day trip, no chance for sightseeing."

She snorted. "I know what you do on these things. You drop package, then spend all day in bar. Are you going to leave me here, alone? It is bad enough when you are here. I am so alone all the time, in a house I do not even like. I am too embarrassed to bring friend over. Please take me with you. Would mean so much."

The desire to be alone struggled in Cal's mind with the desperate need to keep Polina happy. He considered one response after another, went through excuses in his head: the importance of the trip, the length of the car ride, perhaps even faking an illness. Each was less plausible than the last, and the idea of simply putting his foot down and forbidding her from coming along was even less viable. At least he gave a weary nod in her direction.

Polina let out a shriek and jumped out of her recliner. She dashed over and enveloped him in a hug. And for a single moment, it felt like they were in love again.

❋ ❋ ❋

The hotel they stayed at in Atlanta was nice. Nothing too swanky, but still a clean, cheerful suite at a local franchise of a national chain. And for once, Polina did not complain. She had a list of sites to visit, both the usual tourist stuff and more obscure destinations. She woke Cal up early their first morning after a late drive the night before, already dressed in a miniskirt and ridiculously oversized visor.

"First, we must go to aquarium, then Coca-Cola world, then historic mansion I found on website. Then for lunch, I think we go to Murphy's. Can go elsewhere if you like."

Cal shook himself with irritation and stifled his desire to tell her to shut up and let him sleep. He fixed a sleepy grin on his face and attempted a tone of contrition. "I can't do any of that with you, honeybun. I need to work."

Her face fell slightly. "But I thought we spend time together?"

"Tonight. This is a work trip, and Cal's gotta work today, all right?"

She looked dejected and grumpy, but she gave a noise in the affirmative and kissed him on the forehead. "I will go alone, da? Dinner tonight, you promised."

He nodded as she backed out of the room. He checked the clock and swore. Six a.m. He didn't need to be anywhere until eleven. He texted Adam but got no response.

Where Cal needed to be, after going back to sleep, an extended shower, and a late room-service breakfast, was a hotel and convention center downtown. Normally he approached these drops with an almost detached boredom, but in this case, he was nervous. Not only because he had been given the task directly from the boss with the implication that his life was on the line, but because he had never had to do a drop in a big public place like this. Normally it was some non-descript shell of an office. But this was a luxury place topped with a penthouse suite, where Fortune 500 companies held yearly retreats and major trade shows took place. It wasn't just that there were too many witnesses. It was that it all seemed above Cal's pay grade, and Adam still was not answering his texts.

Nevertheless, he got in his car and drove over. He searched for a spot to no avail, before finally gritting his teeth and paying for parking near the top of the attached garage. Still no response from Adam, and as he got out holding his bag, a hard drive full of who knows what stashed in the bottom, he began to dread the possibility that this was all a setup.

But as soon as he closed the car door his cell phone rang from a number he didn't recognize. He put it to his ear, and before he had a chance to speak a low voice was giving Cal instructions.

"You are to go to the Cavalier Ballroom," the voice said. It was clipped and masculine, and distinctly American. Cal thought it sounded familiar. "Tell the guard your name. He will tell you where to go once you are inside. Move quickly. Do not make us wait."

"Hey, wait?"

The call disconnected, and Cal quickly moved toward the elevator. Somehow his anxiety increased even further.

The Cavalier Ballroom was on the basement level, off a side hallway. The only signage indicating it was in use was a sign reading "Closed for Private Event." Outside stood two massive men on either side of the door in plain black suits, one fair and one dark, both completely inscrutable.

The fair one held his hand up as Cal approached and pointed at the sign, slowly shaking his head. Cal looked down at his polo, khaki pants, and loafers, and gave a dark chuckle. Whatever he was getting into, he wasn't dressed for the occasion.

"Terribly sorry, fellas," he said. "My name is Calvin Singer, and I'm here to see Adam."

"There's no Adam," said the darker one. "Please leave."

"Well, I was told to give my name. Could you at least ask?"

The fair one stared for several minutes with what Cal recognized as military intensity. Finally, he slowly spoke into a radio and listened through an earpiece. At last he nodded, and waved Cal forward.

"You're to go to the senator's table," he said. "He is speaking. Do not approach until he is done, or you will be removed from the building. Got it?"

Cal's mouth went dry, and he nodded. *Senator?*

The door opened, and he stepped inside. About a hundred tables, each seating five or six people in breezy daytime suits and summer dresses, were arranged around the ballroom. The lights were turned low, and behind the stage was a large screen with a logo and several lines of text projected onto it. Cal squinted and managed to read it out to himself. *Clean Water Defense Fund Luncheon. Guest Speaker: Senator Thomas Armstrong.*

That name. Armstrong. The name associated with those files that kept appearing time and again on the hard drives. And suddenly the reality, the enormity of what his job entailed, came crashing down upon him in heavy waves of panic.

The only reason he didn't flee right then was the warning he had received about not disturbing the senator's speech. He was going on in a pleasant Southern drawl, one that Cal recognized from some dim memory of a television interview. This Armstrong was hardly a known quantity outside of political junkies. He was a junior senator yet middle-aged, with no strong policy convictions. He was a functionary, an also-ran. Most Americans wouldn't know who this guy was.

"And in conclusion," he was saying, "I hope that we can all redouble our efforts to preserve clean drinking water here in our beautiful country, and work together with the businesses that form the backbone of our communities to leave a brighter future for those to come. I know some might say it's a wash—" and here he paused for a laugh at his weak pun "—but I truly believe we can move forward, together. It's going to take all our hands to get it done, just like how me and my brothers would work that old well pump. Thank you for your time, may God bless you, and may God bless the United States of America."

He nodded and sat back down just off the stage. The applause was polite and loud but just short of rousing. The effect overall was one of deep respect, but it was clear even to a political novice like Cal that Armstrong was a B+ player.

Cal steeled himself and began to pick his way through the tables, slowly progressing towards the table where the senator was seated. On the stage some functionary was making announcements, finishing things up, and waiters moved plates of Georgia peaches and whipped cream from off tables and into waiting bins. They gave Cal annoyed looks as he moved past, but he ignored them.

When he got to the table, another security officer stopped him. He leaned in and repeated his name, and the officer nodded and reached out, taking the bag from his hands. Cal felt a wave of relief and turned to go, but the officer placed a hand on Cal's arm and guided him back to the table, to a chair between a man with dirty blond hair and the senator himself. The guard forced him down, then turned away.

"You should be honored," whispered the blond man. It was Adam. He placed an arm around Cal and smiled. "Then again, I'd be nervous too, if I were you." He reached over and tapped Armstrong on the arm. "Senator, this is Cal. He's one of my employees."

The senator looked surprised, but he shook Cal's hand. "Pleased to meet you. You live in Georgia?"

"Afraid not," Cal squeaked, barely audible.

The emcee called an end to the event and the lights came up. Armstrong clapped politely then stood and turned back to Cal. "Well, good. That means I don't have to worry about your vote." He patted Cal's shoulder. "Take care of this one, Adam. I like him."

Adam nodded, still smiling. "Pleasure to see you as always, Senator."

❀ ❀ ❀

They stood in the elevator, shoulder to shoulder. Cal and Adam. It had been a long time since he had spoken to his boss. He smelled of the right amount of cologne and smiled pleasantly. But his eyes were dead and cold. Out of all the cutthroats and roughnecks he'd met in his time, Adam scared Cal the most.

"You're in a lot of trouble," Adam said. Even now his voice was light and even-tempered. "I don't know what you did to Sokolov, but he's not too pleased. But then again, you are also incredibly lucky. He doesn't clue many people in to the extent of his business. As his son-in-law, I suppose it was only a matter of time."

Cal unstuck his dry, fattened tongue. "We do business with senators? I thought it was just PACs. I thought I was meddling with little state campaigns so we could save money on shipping costs."

"It was. But every business must grow or wither away. Now we do business directly with campaigns. I am sure you have realized that we operate as independent cells? Well, then, there is a bit of competition, you understand. Previously, it was only Patriot Solutions that dealt with Congress. But I have ambition, Calvin Singer. So, I started to make inroads from my region. And now it's paid off."

"I don't imagine Eva is happy with your horning in on her territory."

"Eva doesn't have what it takes to run this long term; I do. Armstrong is a huge get, let me tell you. First one on this scale. We have our eyes set on the 2016 presidential election, but we'll have to see who runs. For now, this will have to do. And it's doing well. See, this Armstrong, he's not much to look at. Not a lot of charisma. If one of his friends at the Rotary Club hadn't introduced him to me, he would have been labeled a do-nothing state legislator. But with our help, he made it through the primary, and we did away with the opposition in the general. Now he's angling for bigger things. Senate leadership, cabinet positions. All on the back of what we can supply him and what we can do to his opponents. Let me just say, from the bottom of my heart, thank you Calvin Singer. Without your information, I could never have ingratiated myself this deeply with Armstrong. You're far better at this than Matt ever was."

"If you wanted to give me a performance review, we could have done that back in Jackson."

"This isn't a review, Calvin Singer. This is a promotion. You should be honored."

"You'll understand if I'm a bit shocked that I've been fucking with the United States Senate. Especially after you told me not to believe Eva."

"Did you honestly think that our operation was so small? I wanted to see what you would do. If you would be so foolish as to try and run. But you didn't and I would commend you if I hadn't spent an hour last week getting screamed at by Sokolov over how disappointed he is in you. Apparently, you may be unfit to be married to his daughter. Therefore, I do not mix family and business."

"Long elevator ride."

"Oh, we're going to the penthouse. Do you know why Sokolov lives in a piss-poor village, Cal? It's not because he can't afford better, it's because he owns the whole freaking village. If Putin's men or CIA dogs came looking for him, every person in Breznygrad would lay down their lives for him."

"Even you?"

Adam smiled. "I'm not in Breznygrad." The doors opened. "After you, Calvin Singer."

The penthouse was really something. There was no bed to see, of course, just a spacious great room with a marble fireplace and expansive glass windows offering a fantastic view of the skyline. The sky had darkened since Cal arrived, and it threatened to storm, giving the room an ominous vibe. Several white couches were arranged around the lowered floor, each holding at least one guy in a suit, and in the middle, tied to the chair and gagged, was another man.

Cal swallowed the golf ball–size lump that had formed in his throat as he felt his heart rate accelerate and his face developed a stone-cold stare and he could hear his own heartbeat in his head. He wondered what he was about to be told to do. Adam had positioned himself directly behind Cal's right side, gently placing his hand on his left shoulder, he leaned into Cal's right ear.

"The single greatest requirement for one to rise through the ranks," he said quietly, "is loyalty."

Adam waved a hand. One of the guys got up and set up a small video camera and tripod aimed right at the prisoner.

"I don't think you understand what you're involved in," Adam said. "I tried to tell you, did I not? Show up on time. Drop the fake Southern charm act. Learn how to spend your money. But did you listen to me? No, you just kept on. You scrimped and saved and wore that stupid grin every day of your life. Well now it has finally caught up with you. If you haven't been able to show us what you are worth, then I will have to provide the pressure that will reveal what you truly are. And if not that, then the pain."

The air smelled of blood and vodka.

"We can do whatever we want here, and not a single person in this hotel is going to say a word. Did you think this was some small-time gangster shit? Poor Calvin. In less than a decade, we will buy and sell presidents on the back of the work you've done for us. Don't you want to be a part of something more? You told me you had ambition. I thought you knew your place. Your place is here. This is the price of your ambition."

The prisoner's eyes locked with Cal. He pleaded wordlessly, but they both knew it was too late.

"What do you want me to do?" Cal asked. "Shoot him? Interrogate him?"

Adam laughed. "We don't shoot people unless we have to. And I would not trust interrogating anyone to a man as incompetent as you. No. You were discharged from the Army for breaking a man's arm, correct? What a trashy thing to do. You must have one hell of a right hook." He got so close to Cal their faces almost touched. "I want you to beat this man until he stops moving."

Cal shook his head. "This isn't in my job description."

"Did that sound like a question? My mistake. Beat this man until he stops moving. Or I will beat you both, until you both stop moving."

Adam stepped away. There was nothing for it. There was no negotiating, no better option. Whatever Cal expected; it had not been this. The enormity of it all threatened to overwhelm him, but he managed to keep it together. The ultimatum was simple: kill a stranger or die. Who was this guy to Cal? Just some nut. He was doomed as it was. Upon closer inspection Cal could already see blood on the man's shirt and the rug. The only possible response was to shed more of it.

Cal stepped forward. The prisoner stared at him, hope draining away. Cal raised his fist and brought it down across the man's face.

❋ ❋ ❋

He sat in his car for a full half hour. Adam had given him a change of clothes and actually shaken his hand, welcomed him to the next level. There were jokes about pay raises, but Cal was too deeply in shock to say anything at all. That was fine by Adam. He just clapped him on the back and warned him casually about the tape. They hadn't made Cal check the prisoner's pulse, but they didn't have to.

There was no way to block this out of his mind, try as he might. Cal was a murderer now. All through his years of violence, he had never killed a man. For the first time in his life he felt true regret, a genuine outpouring of remorse that made him sob bitter tears. Polina kept calling his cell phone, but he ignored it, too ashamed and frightened to answer. Cal faded away into his childhood memories, remembering how much simpler life really was back then. He thought he hated the life he'd had in Owensboro, but now, now it didn't look so bad. His few old high school hang-out buddies he'd left behind years ago would likely never see him again, not even at the high school reunion, his new life as a criminal would surely force him into being a loner, maybe even into hiding. Cal had no idea what was about to happen next, but he knew he was now a murderer.

The question was what to do now. He had heard that it got easier, and he had no doubt that it would. But did he want it to? If he stayed, if he stayed with Polina and continued to work for Sokolov and Adam, then surely, he would kill again. What if Polina's patience ran out and dumped him, where would that put him with Sokolov? Would he now be the target of some new trainee? His mind wondered, unsettling to say the least.

His phone rang once more. He took it out and stared at it. There was blood under his nails. He had another choice, one that would need to be exercised with the utmost care. He would have to pretend it was all business as usual as he set everything up. It would take a cooler head than he'd yet exhibited, but he knew he could do it.

As he lifted the phone to his ear and heard Polina's stern admonitions about his lateness, Cal knew he had to run away.

Ten

The therapist sat cross-legged in what looked like a very comfortable chair, wearing short hair and a conservative tweed skirt that seemed too warm for the Mississippi heat. Her office was a riot of condescending feel-good bullshit. The flowers, seemingly there to provide a calming effect, were obviously plastic and in need of a good dusting. There was a small bookshelf packed with self-help. *The Purpose-Driven Life, Chicken Soup for the Car Mechanic's Soul, Inside Baseball: Base Running Your Way to a Better You.* None of the books appeared to have been even glanced through. On the left-hand side wall facing the door hung a massive poster of a garish cat on a tree branch. The caption read "You Can Do It!" Apparently "Hang in There" was taken.

But Cal needed this. It seemed that Adam had reported back favorably to Sokolov. The boss man hadn't bothered Cal since, and the general air of their communications seemed to imply that Cal had entered a new level of their relationship. Now and again, Cal would get random emails from unknown addresses simply signed "A" that offered glimpses into the true nature of his work. There were oblique mentions of the need for encryption and various districts where elections were being held, unmistakable references to high-ranking figures of both political parties, government jargon and acronyms Cal hadn't seen since his security credentials had been revoked. Even as he was attempting to separate himself from this world of crime, he'd found himself in, Cal was being plunged deeper into an even more disturbing world of espionage.

But that was before the nightmares began. Every night in the weeks since he came back from Atlanta had been one image of horror after another. Not just the unfortunate prisoner, either. He spent hours tossing and turning as graphic movies of corpses in far-off places he had never seen played before his eyes. It made sleep impossible, so much so that Polina had insisted he either get himself fixed or sleep on the couch. But the couch just made it worse, and he was losing so much sleep that not only was his work for Sokolov of lower quality than it had ever been, but he couldn't even make any preparations for his now inevitable escape from the Russians. So as much as he abhorred psychologists of every kind, he found himself signing up for therapy. Just enough to maybe get some medicine and have a quick chat about how much it sucked to watch yourself beat a man to death over and over every night.

"So, Calvin," the therapist began. By her voice he'd guess she came from Chicago. "Can I call you Calvin?"

"It's Cal, actually," he said. He wanted to make a crack about being called "Mr. Singer" but didn't have the energy.

Her face brightened with an artificial smile. "Cal. Nice name. Like Cal Ripken. Are you a baseball fan?"

"Not really into sports."

She seemed disappointed but went on. "Well, my name is Naomi. It's a pleasure to meet you. I am a very well trained and experienced psychotherapist, a counselor if you will. I am here to mostly listen and help you in any way I can. What we are going to do is I'm going to ask you a few questions and you're going to give me a few answers, and together we can maybe help you through this emotional challenge you're going through right now, okay? This is completely confidential, no one will know you are here or why you are here, unless I believe you are an imminent threat to others or a threat to yourself. Does that sound all right to you?"

"Fine. Just want the nightmares to stop."

Naomi immediately began scribbling on a yellow legal pad. "What kind of nightmares?"

Cal opened his mouth to speak, but suddenly found that he could not. The words to describe what he saw every night escaped him. It was like someone had balled up a sock and put it in his mouth. He closed his mouth and stared at her, furious at his own dumb silence.

Naomi reached onto her desk and picked up his file, briskly rifling through it. "Says here you're a veteran. Is that correct?"

Cal nodded.

"Were you in Iraq?"

Cal didn't say anything, just looked at her.

Naomi sighed. "Let me tell you a bit more about what I specialize in, and we can go from there. I mostly work with those who suffer from trauma. I have seen a lot of different kinds of people. Rape survivors, victims of child abuse. A lot of veterans. There are many approaches we can take to process this, and I won't know which is right for you at first. Therapy is not a quick thing. It can take many years and a lot of hard work. But we can talk until you feel comfortable giving me some details. Is that okay?"

It didn't seem okay to Cal. What he wanted was to get his head right as quickly as possible, not spend years in some terrible office environment talking to a woman with a mouth full of chewing gum, popping it about every third or fourth chew all the while sucking on one of those awful smelling vaporizers. This Naomi had no sense of urgency.

"What do you want me to tell you, Doc?" Cal said. "I got a lot going on up here."

"Maybe just start with how you're feeling."

Cal laughed, an honest belly laugh, enough volume for him to scare himself. "How am I feeling? Well, let's see, my wife, she's the worst. Just the absolute worst. Doesn't appreciate me at all. I work for her father, and that's a hot mess because he wants me to slave away for his baby girl, but I ain't good at that either. I got no family to speak of, and the goddamn VA sucks, it's of no use to me. So, I'm feeling great, Doc. I'm feeling like a million goddamn bucks, to tell you the truth."

Naomi scribbled furiously. Something told Cal he shouldn't have started with Polina. "OK, back up. Is your wife appearing in your nightmares?"

"No."

"Is her father?"

"No, but the guys that work for him sure do. While we are here, let me just say I'm not going to talk about my job. At all."

"Very well." She finished scribbling and looked up at Cal. "But if they're appearing in your nightmares, they seem related."

Her words from earlier returned to Cal. *Threat to yourself or others.* If he told her the truth, she would have the police officers on him so fast he wouldn't make it to the parking lot. And once Sokolov or, worse, Adam found out he was compromised, well, that would be the end of Calvin Singer. He wouldn't even make it to trial. Adam would have some goon with a neck like a ham cut his throat and make it look like a suicide.

The options were to either confess to the therapist and die in prison or abandon the whole thing and steadily decline to the point where he would be killed anyway. Cal wondered idly if death was a viable option. It couldn't be too bad, right? He didn't have any faith left, so there was no thought of hell on his mind. It would be like an endless, dreamless sleep. He would have peace for the first time in his life, something he had never gotten from Sokolov, or Polina, or his hometown, and definitely not those bastards in the Army.

And as he thought of the Army, a solution occurred to Cal.

"You know what, Doc?" He leaned forward in his chair. "To hell with all of it. I'm going to tell you what happened."

Naomi sat back, surprised. "Go on, then."

"I didn't see a lot of action in Iraq." There was one thing Cal knew he was good at, besides fighting, and that was spinning a yarn to get what he wanted. "By the time I got there, all the big stuff had already gone down. We were mostly there to secure the place, do some training, help the locals get their shit together. So, they posted me out at some godforsaken village a few klicks away from Fallujah, just on the edge of the green zone. The locals, they are all goat herders, real simple people. And the place has just been wrecked. They had some Al Qaeda that moved in after Saddam fell, but our boys had already pushed those sons of bitches out. So besides like building schools and making sure no one came by and stole all their goats, we were supposed to be making sure these Islamist thugs didn't come back in and kidnap all the girls for learning how to read."

Naomi's expression softened a bit at the mention of women and children. "Sounds like a noble thing you were doing."

"Well, we thought so anyway. The good news is that for the most part it was quiet. See, at that point the militias, they were not really fighting for anything. They were basically street gangs, bandits, roaming around, taking over villages and stealing all their shit, capping a few of the men and stealing the prettiest girls. They'd use these places to move drugs and weapons, and they wouldn't wear any insignia so they could blend in." Cal didn't really know a damn thing about Iraq. He just wanted to sell her a good lie. "You'd get these hotheaded boys in the villages who'd basically be the local toughs, trying to run their game right under our noses. Every now and again someone would disappear, and we wouldn't know if it was because they were Al Qaeda who ran off, scared, or if they'd been killed by some militia rat we hadn't managed to chase out."

Cal paused for effect. Naomi was on the edge of her seat, chewing on her pen.

"OK, so one day Sarge tells us we're going to do a sweep. Go house to house, interrogate these guys, see if anyone showed up in the middle of the night with a kilo of heroin. We check out the first couple places, arrest a few guys so we can give them a pat down and have a chat. They are all clean. By the time we get to the fifth place, we know something is wrong. Nobody answers the door, but we can hear movement. We breach, and I see a target. Raise my weapon. Fire."

Here, Cal felt the balled-up sock again. He was about to weave in some truth.

"And when the smoke clears, there's two dead Al Qaeda holding AKs. But in the middle of the room there is this guy tied to a chair with a bullet wound in his chest. And he is just all messed up. He didn't look like a person anymore. Whatever they did to him, he wasn't in any kind of shape to move by the time we got there."

Unbidden tears rose to Cal's eyes. The image of the hotel room in Atlanta floated before him, and he covered his face.

Naomi reached out and patted his arm. "I'm so sorry."

"I think, sometimes, that I'd actually put him out of his misery. What kind of a life is it when you've got half a face? But then again, I killed that guy. He's dead, because of me."

"And the people you work with. They appear in your recollections of this?"

"It's a mess. It's all a mess. Everything just jumbles in my mind."

Now came the real waterworks. The story was a lie, but the pain was real. Cal thought telling her a lie would work like it always did. That it would get him what he wanted and alleviate his own stress. But all it really did was make him hate himself even more for using someone else's story for his own purposes.

"What do you do for a living, Cal?"

He looked up to her through tears. It would feel good to tell the truth, if only a part of it. "Cybersecurity."

It was not clear if she bought it, but Naomi pretended to in any case. "So, the war is still real for you. Even if you're fighting with computers now."

Cal nodded, but there was no relief for him. He couldn't tell where the lies ended, and the truth began. He spent the rest of his hour sobbing, reaching for words and not grasping them, as the therapist cooed soft and empty reassurances into his ear.

"Mr. Singer, Cal, I'm going to write a recommendation for a prescription and send it over to your personal physician. Something to settle your nerves a bit and another to help you sleep, let's talk again next Thursday, okay? I'll ask your doctor to approve and issue the prescription to your pharmacy and have them drop you a text when it's ready to be picked up, that okay with you?"

"Great, thanks"

✿✿✿

The bar at The Mermaid was mercifully almost empty. Cal sat alone, staring mindlessly at early-evening Sports Center, barely wetting his lips with a glass of Jim Beam as the sun's reddening light streamed in through the front windows, reflecting off the lake as it sank behind the trees.

Brian was polishing the rims of wine glasses and restocking the beer cooler in between telling a story to a lone customer, about his buddy's cigarette boat and how incredibly fast it was. It would be dinnertime soon, and people would be languidly filing in to fill themselves up with fish and shrimp, baked potatoes, cold beer or good wine. For a moment, Cal dreamt of a normal life with a day job. He was planning on cutting out before then, but that also depended on how his mental state would change over the next hour. He had gotten his two prescriptions filled and popped one of nerve pills in his mouth and washed it down with a big gulp of Jameson.

Naomi had given Cal some "homework" as she called it, a term that irritated him. She wanted a list of times he felt a strong negative emotional shift throughout the week. He had been so worn out he couldn't explain to her that every day was a strong negative emotional shift.

He pulled his laptop out of his bag and laid it down on the bar. Brian frowned a bit but said nothing. Working in a bar wasn't nearly that odd of a thing to do, was it? Either way, Cal had lost what interest he'd ever had in propriety as soon as his fist landed on that poor bastard's face. He shook his head to banish the image and opened the folder where he hid the most important computer files he had ever handled.

Every single drive he'd gotten his hands on since he had realized the full scope of all this, Cal had made a copy of, hidden in a flash drive image. To the outsider, it would look like he was just making recovery drives for a web server, even though he was stashing blackmail. The things on those drives could take down half the state and local governments all over the South, and that wasn't even counting the number of congressmen, senators, White House officials, candidates, and operatives he'd glanced the names and faces of. It was mostly just dry, boring stuff about voter rolls and personal lives, insider information on how campaigns were being run. But occasionally, Cal happened upon something revolting, an image of an illicit sex act or some evidence of embarrassing, possibly criminal activity.

The plan was simple: sell the house. That would give him a decent chunk of cash on top of what he had managed to squirrel away. The house was in his name only, and Polina did not have access to his rathole bank account nor did she realize that he had one. Then he would send some of these materials to certain people in law enforcement, with the understanding that he had the rest of it. If they wanted to leak them, if they wanted to buy the rest of them, if they wanted him to remain silent until the end of time, that was fine with Calvin Singer. The only thing he wanted was an assurance that they would not come for him.

Or maybe he was looking at this the wrong way. The world was not split into Russians and Americans. There would have to be someone, some tin-pot dictator, crime lord, or up-and-coming rogue state that would love to get their hands on this. Forget about getting assurances. Perhaps he could make his fortune off this, pick up a few million dollars and retire like a king. What did he care what they did with it? The world was bigger than North America, and surely somewhere Cal could find people that would treat him as he deserved to be treated.

No matter what path he chose, he would have to make physical copies and stash them in the house until the time was right. Sending them digitally would leave a far bigger digital paper trail than just dropping flash drives in random mailboxes. Maybe he'd rat them out to the news as well, really drop a big scandal on all of them. Cal felt a certain perverse glee at the idea of compromising the entire electoral system of the United States. From what he could tell, this had become a pervasive practice, and candidates from damn near every state south of the Mason-Dixon was employing Revolver in some capacity. That rinky-dink little operation in a low-rise office building in Jackson was the heart of a scandal that would undo America as they all knew it.

And good riddance too, Cal thought. He thought back to Eva, calling them both citizens of the world. The Americans were a bunch of decadent slobs, men and women with false honor who didn't care who they trod upon. They hadn't given him a damn thing, and in the process, they had driven him into the bosom of what was left of the spirit, if not the machine, of their sleeping enemy.

But the Russians, oh those Russians. How was it they were even worse? To force Cal to do what he had done in that hotel room. And Adam had just stood there, watching silently. He had been, as always, the absolute picture of poise, a vision of competence. His eyes had remained icy and solid, uncaring about the human costs of his actions. It was clear that the only thing he cared about was the business. Or maybe he thought of it as the mission. He was bringing about a new world, whether he realized it or not.

If anything, Cal believed the Americans deserved what they had coming. They would be taken apart if ever the full scope of

Sokolov's organization was exposed. How many cells were there, after all? Just the Revolver-style fake companies, let alone all the other corruption, the payoffs, the overt profit-driven criminality that he was surely engaging in stateside. The Americans had helped him, if anything. They had gotten mixed up in him, had failed to keep an eye on the businesses that were set up in their neighborhoods. Adam's smug face floated before Cal again. Of course, that was all they needed: a pretty face, something to set them at ease. Did the Americans even know what it meant to be an American? To toil in obscurity. To be raised in some unknown town in Kentucky, then to give up years of your life to defend it for nothing. Backpacking across the country, going from job to job with no sign of it ever getting better. No, Cal would be only too happy to watch the chaos from afar.

As for where he would go, he had not decided yet. It would not be possible to stay in country, of course. Cal would need to go abroad, somewhere they wouldn't extradite him. Treason prosecutions never went well, and Cal himself would be found guilty in the court of public opinion in no time. An anti-American fuck-up, a dishonorably discharged veteran who had gone over to a foreign power over hurt pride to get revenge? It would be a miracle if he wasn't killed on the spot. It would be better to be long gone before it all blew up. Preferably someplace warm, with friendly and beautiful women who could soothe his ego and banish the image of his victim from his eyeballs and his brain. Maybe at last he could be free of that poor man's caved-in face and pleading eyes that blamed him every night for what Cal had taken away from him.

There was no way he could face Polina in this state. Cal was honestly frightened of what he could do to her. It was like a seal had been broken, and now he was aware of what his fists could really do. Violence and death had become real in a way he had never experienced before. Until Atlanta, getting into a rumble with someone was almost sport. It was just something that happened when the tension got too high. But now things had changed.

He hadn't been able to articulate much else, after the fake war story reduced Cal to a blubbering idiot. He managed to deflect her questions about what his job entailed with vague references to cybersecurity, and for the most part Naomi was satisfied, if suspicious. But there now existed a very real threat of being ratted out, and as Cal sat in The Mermaid, he couldn't help but let his thoughts of violence stray toward her as well.

He had killed one person. Had he enlisted in the military at virtually any other time in American history, it seemed likely that he would be expected to kill even more. The long, proud warrior tradition didn't condemn righteous violence. In the name of defense, the deaths of others were considered a justified, if not unfortunate expense. It was them, or us. And as a man without a country, could he really be expected not to defend himself? Not to take what action was needed to ensure his continued survival? No man could be expected to lie down and die like a kicked dog. Calvin Singer was now a Patriot to no one and no country.

❈ ❈ ❈

An entire arsenal was hidden in that closet. When he purchased the first weapon, it had been just for sport. It was nice to have a sporting rifle. But then he bought another, and another. And it wasn't just rifles, either. Body armor, entry shotguns, grenade launchers. After a while he realized that he wasn't just arming himself because it was fun. He was waiting for something, an inevitable explosion when he would be forced to defend himself. It might be the Russians. Might be the feds. But part of him had always known someone would come for him.

His cell phone rang. It was Polina. Cal steeled himself and picked up.

"Where are you?" she asked. Her tone was short and brutal already, but less so than usual. "We are supposed to go to dinner."

"I'm at The Mermaid. Therapy ran a bit long. Was thinking we could eat here?"

"Mermaid? Why? We always go there."

Cal didn't want to admit it, but things between them had improved as of late. Ever since what Polina had seen as a brief working vacation and the pending sale of the house, she'd been in a better mood. To her, the idyllic Southern lifestyle she'd lusted after for so long was within her grasp, only a few moments away. She had been so excited she barely registered her husband's growing quietness, the way he would stare off and say nothing while they sat on the couch, that he was spending almost all his time in his study. Polina just assumed he was hard at work bringing her what she deserved. She could not imagine how close Cal was to an exit, or worse, opening the back wall of the closet.

"I don't know, Polina."

"I call you because Harry is here."

Cal sat up, alert. "Harry? He's not scheduled to come around."

"He want to see house again. Said he want to think about remodel. I tell him I will not let him inside without my husband. Very rude man."

A trickle of paranoia crept down Cal's spine. He hung up the phone, threw down some cash, and grabbed his car keys. He needed that house sold. Pocketing that money was essential if he wanted to escape.

Eleven

*H*arry had been perfectly polite when he knocked on the door and explained why he'd come around.

"Terribly sorry for bothering you, Mrs. Singer," he began, "but I was wondering if it wouldn't be possible to just take the briefest look around one more time? I'm already making plans about a possible renovation, see, and I wanted to have a good picture for what needed work when I speak to my contractor tomorrow."

"Why are you here?" Polina had asked. "You should not be here. My husband is not home. You will not come in while my husband is not home."

"Well, again, I'm quite sorry to come by unannounced. If you don't mind, I'll look around outside?"

Polina had just grunted and shut the door. Harry took that as a yes.

Their relationship puzzled Harry. He hadn't been able to learn any details about the couple besides the fact that she was a Russian national with no other ties to the U.S. Her maiden name, Popov, set off no alarm bells. There weren't any oligarchs with that name. It made sense with Harry's working theory that she was a mail-order bride. But hadn't Cal said something about his father-in-law being his employer? Was that a cover story, or was it just a coincidence? It seemed possible that there was nothing genuinely troubling about the Singers at all, that they were just a couple gun-nut oddballs who argued constantly.

There was a neighbor outside, washing his BMW convertible. He waved to Harry, who waved back with a big smile. He was tempted to walk over and talk to him, but he knew Polina would be watching. If the Russian wasn't suspicious already, she would be if he started to interrogate the other people on their street. He decided to come back another time and made note of the house number in his phone so he could research the man's name for later.

The boys back at the Company got excited when Harry mentioned the arsenal stashed in the study. To them, that was absolute proof that everything was not aboveboard with Calvin Singer. Harry wasn't so sure. He had not gotten inside Cal's head yet enough to make a judgement call, and he didn't want to make unverified accusations. To him, there was nothing inherently wrong with an American owning a few firearms. That was his constitutional right. What really made him uneasy was the body armor. It didn't seem like the kind of thing someone would keep around unless they planned on getting shot at.

He decided to take a close look at the power meter. It looked like there was a significant draw, which made sense considering what he knew about Cal's line of work. The study had played host to quite a bit of computer equipment. Then again, Harry could not help but wonder if that didn't bode well for the air conditioning system or how well the home was insulated. Harry really liked the place, besides whatever other interests The Company had in it. He genuinely felt that it would be the perfect fit for him, but reminded himself that there was other work to do. He would have to broach the subject of a buying the place from The Company later. For now, this would have to wait.

He strolled around the back and found the outside cable box. It only took him a moment to pick the lock and open it up. Once he did, he let out a low whistle. As he expected, there had been some adjustments made. He had a feeling no one from the local company had come by to inspect the hook-up. If they had, they would have noticed the wires and devices plugged into the thing, all of them designed to further confound any enterprising counterintelligence agents looking to sniff around Cal's data.

He took a tiny device out of his pocket and tried to remember how to attach it. Telecommunications was not his area of expertise—buildings were. He managed to get it turned on, but he was unsure how exactly to attach it to the spaghetti of wires Cal had stuck in this thing.

He heard an engine coming and dashed around, peeking out the side of the house. Cal's orange Hummer was coming up the street.

Harry cursed and ran back—of course the Russian would call her husband. Working faster than he had a in a long time, he finally managed to get the thing attached and got the box shut, fitting the lock back in just as the Hummer's engine cut off and the driver's side door slammed shut.

He came around the corner of the house, smiling widely, but stopped short as he saw Cal. The guy did not look good. He'd lost at least ten pounds since they'd seen each other last and was an entire shade whiter.

Composing himself, Harry held out a hand. "Pleasure to see you. Sorry about scaring the wife like that."

Cal took his hand and shook it weakly. There was a dead look in his eye. "Don't worry about her. She's always mad about something. You came to take another look at the place? I hope you're not planning on backing out?" His grip tightened.

Harry looked him in the eye. "The opposite, actually; I'm getting so excited about getting in this place that I just wanted to take another look around. I'd like to make a few adjustments and really make it my own, you understand." He felt his cell phone buzz in his pocket.

Cal nodded. "You can come in, if you like." He finally let go of Harry's hand.

"That's nice of you, but I'm afraid I spooked Polina. I'd rather come back another day, if it's all the same. I just took a quick look around the property, thinking of maybe adding copper gutters. What do you think?"

"Gutters. Right. Well, no doubt they would add a bit more sparkle to the street appeal, just give me a call, we can hook up almost any time that I'm in town."

"Right. Hey, look Cal, how does the middle of April sound for a closing date, that's just two weeks away, is that too soon for you? There is a huge tax credit offered by the IRS if I purchase and close by April 15th, I'd really like to cash in on that credit if possible."

Cal's eyes bugged a little as he rubbed his chin. "Uh well, I am in a hurry but that's sooner than I had planned for, as I haven't actually made a deal on a new place yet. Okay, so what if we closed then but you allowed me to rent it back from you for a month or so, would that work for you? I'll take out renters' insurance to protect your investment if you want."

"Sure, I can deal with that," Harry responded. "I'll have my agent draw up the docs and set the date, I'll be back in touch soon."

"Great, so that settles it, I'm all excited now Harry, I just can't wait, and I know my wife will be elated"

Back in his truck Harry took a deep breath. Something wasn't right with Cal; he could sense it. When they met, he merely seemed stressed, a coarse, wound-up ball of anxiety. But now he had the look of a desperate man. A man who could do anything. Maybe there was more to all this than he had originally thought. Maybe bullets were heading Cal's way.

Twelve

The low-rise office building wasn't much to look at. It had been built for the sake of economy, not style, and was altogether unremarkable in every way. There was nothing about it that identified with or referenced the surrounding city of Jackson, nothing to set it apart from the dozens and dozens of comparable structures Harry had seen or even worked on in his time building and developing commercial real estate. It was just another anonymous collection of concrete and glass, timeless but somehow already dated. It was exactly the kind of place, Harry thought to himself, that would be ideal if you were trying to hide some sort of illegal activity from prying federal government eyes.

Going into this, he was not sure what he'd expected. He had jumped at the chance to come back to his own neck of the woods at the direction of the Company. There were ulterior motives at play here, of course: he had not been lying when he told Cal that he'd been looking for a nice spot to settle down in, now that his days of hopping around were coming to an end. It was just that his interest in this particular house wasn't based purely on speculation about his own future.

He had gotten the call about Cal a few months back. The Company had kept him on retainer for almost a year now, specifically looking for his area of expertise and offering him a chance to ply his skills to serve his country. Technically he was an independent contractor for a real estate speculation firm out of Tallahassee, which in turn was kept on retainer by the State Department. It was generally dull stuff: they'd bring him in to inspect suspicious buildings, do information gathering on projects headed up by shady foreign investors, procure assets that would be turned over to bland, serious men who wore heavy off-the-rack suits in sweltering Mississippi heat.

So, when they told him to contact Cal, it was odd to say the least. After all, Harry was a commercial real estate guy, not residential. And besides, what was the deal with this dorky computer nerd that made him so interesting? Even after meeting him, Harry thought the whole thing was a waste of time. Some odd bit of information must have set something off in a file somewhere and that led to his mistimed activation. But that was before he got an eyeful of the body armor and guns, the surplus military equipment, the Russian wife and the odd, nervous energy Cal gave off at every turn.

He had planted the device on Cal's internet uplink at the behest of some egghead or another who wanted to take a closer look. To Harry, the threat was not a digital one. He'd been around for a while. He'd helped the boys from Langley raid enough office complexes to know the difference between a disgruntled hacker who is in too deep and an honest-to-goodness wild card. The ones who poked around where they didn't belong, they were academic types looking to make a quick buck—smart, bored kids with anti-government tendencies who liked to keep their illegal endeavors well abstracted from the dangers they caused in the real world. But guys like Cal were a different story; they hoarded weapons and had fantasies of overthrowing what they saw as illegitimate authority. They were the ones who could go Postal at any moment. And Cal, well, he was wound tighter than a two-dollar watch.

It turned out his read wasn't right this time, though. Harry mopped the sweat from his brow, shook his head, and entered the cool building lobby. Whatever was going between Cal and Russia was bad enough for the boys to send him an encrypted email from a burner account. It was only a few lines: *Go to workplace. Interrogate coworkers.* And then the address and suite number for Cal's place of work. Harry searched Cal's place of work, Revolver Solutions, online before heading in. Sounded like some sort of niche software developer for lumber companies and sawmills, which, if nothing else, fit with Cal's description of his father-in-law's business.

He approached the large black man sitting behind the security desk. The tag on his chest read "JD."

"How you doing'?" Harry asked with a smile. "I'm looking for Revolver Solutions. Sixth floor, right?"

JD looked up, then sat back in his chair. "Revolver. You sure? I never get anyone looking for their office."

"Pretty sure. I have business to discuss with them."

JD chuckled. "Know what? You will be their first business in months. Then again, maybe they do all that by computers nowadays. I don't know. I'm an old-fashioned sort of guy."

Harry leaned forward, smiling conspiratorially. "I'm with you on that one. They're always making us move to some new software or another. Can't keep up anymore."

"You got that right, sir."

"Say, you wouldn't happen to have seen a guy named Calvin Singer come through here today, have you? I know he works at Revolver, was hoping I could say hi."

Suddenly JD's whole demeanor changed, became more hostile. He was no longer relaxed and open. "You a friend of his?"

"Not at all, I hardly know the guy but by an odd coincidence I've been looking at his house. You see, I'm a construction project manager for a large construction firm, and they are relocating me to this area to set up a small project management office somewhere in the area. I've been looking for a place to live nearby. It so happens that Cal's place is up for sale, and it's the first house I've liked, that's how we met.

"I'm here at the request of the building owners, see, to survey some of the spaces for potential remodeling, maybe some structural corrections and mold remediation."

"Structural work, huh?" JD snorted. "Had to shut down half the second-floor last year because they didn't install the exterior sheathing right and there were moisture issues. Well, I hate you had to meet Cal."

"Why?"

"About all I can say about him is he's a good for nothing, so don't quote me on this. He used to work for me about three years back. Never could show up on time, and one day he just walked right out."

"No shit, really? So, if you had to guess, how would a man like that go from a security guard to working at a place like Revolver?"

"Beats me." JD lowered his voice. "I ain't supposed to tell you this, but that boy was dishonorably discharged. Broke an officer's collarbone or something like that."

Harry thought once again of the body armor in Cal's mud room. "You don't say."

"I was glad to be rid of him, to be quite honest with you. He was always a thorn in my side, nothing but trouble, and you know what they say, a leopard don't change his spots. I'd spend as little time around him as you can get by with, mister."

Harry nodded. "So, Revolver?"

"Oh yeah, sorry about that. You got me gossiping and once I start, I don't stop; sixth floor, all the way on the right, can't miss it."

"I appreciate it, thanks." Harry headed to the elevator as the door was opening for an exiting passenger, he stepped on with a few others and punched 6; dazed at what he had just learned. Three years ago, Cal had been a dishonorably discharged security guard at a nondescript office plaza. And now he was a cyber-security expert working for what was probably a subsidiary of a Russian lumber importer, driving a brand-new Hummer, stashing guns and ammo in a house he shouldn't be able to afford. Suddenly he looked a lot more suspicious. *Surely the Company had all this information about Cal on file already, why have they not clued me in,* Harry thought. *I know, it's that paygrade thing again obviously.*

Everyone else on board the elevator got off before the sixth floor, leaving Harry to ride the last two alone. From what he could tell from glimpsing past the doors, the inside of the building was just as mundane as the exterior. But when the doors opened on the top floor, that impression faded a bit. It was hard to identify what was wrong with this one, more of a combination of things than any one particular flaw. The carpet was shabbier, the walls painted a less-appealing color. However long this place had been up, it was clear that floors one through five got more love from maintenance than the sixth did.

Revolver Solutions, it seemed, was not just the door farthest down the right-hand hall. It was the only office on that side of the building, located behind a frosted-glass door with a small name-plate that simply read "Revolver" off to the side. Harry pushed the door open and stepped inside.

"Can I help you?" asked a voice.

Harry turned to face it and found a dumpy young woman with brightly-dyed purple hair, staring up at him from a low, sprawling desk. No less than three computer monitors sat in front of her, and he noticed energy drink cans all over her workspace. Behind her sat a massive copier spitting out papers.

"Hello," Harry said, taken aback. "I'm looking for the office manager?"

The woman took a long pull on a vaporizer and exhaled a noxious cloud of fruit-scented mist, attempting to blow a smoke ring.

Those things always irritated Harry. Smoking was one thing but exhaling like a freight train in someone's face was not only nauseating but uncouth. "Well," she said. "The manager ain't in, I'm afraid. In fact," she added as she swept her arm around the place, "as you can see, nobody's in."

She was right. Harry looked around the place and was shocked at what he saw. It was ostensibly an open-floor-plan office, except instead of desks there was a series of long white folding tables placed seemingly at random. They were stacked mostly with computers of all shapes and sizes, and thick bundles of cable ran all over the place. Overflowing trash buckets stuffed with paper and Mountain Dew bottles were scattered here and there. The face of one entire wall was down, exposing the steel structure and metal framing of the building. It looked less like an office and more like a thrift store that dealt exclusively in high-end electronics.

"I see," Harry said. He was at something of a loss. He imagined the eggheads back in Virginia would have been overjoyed to get their hands on all of this. For his purposes, it was not overly useful.

The receptionist sighed. "Look man, maybe I can help you out. I'm Meryl, and I'm the best you got. Nobody comes to work here more than once a week."

"What exactly do you all do here?"

"If you ask them, they just say, 'We're in the lumber business,' and then run out. Doesn't look like the lumber business to me, but they pay me to answer phones and play *Counterstrike*, not ask probing questions. What do you want with this bunch?"

Harry decided to fall back on the cover story. This Meryl seemed like the trusting type. He could use that. "Well, Meryl, I represent a construction firm that's been contracted by the property owner to look at some structural issues in this building. The building insurer has voiced some concerns, so I'm here to check them out and report back."

They both turned in unison to look at the large opening in the exterior wall.

"Oh, is that why the wall is opened up over there?" Meryl said.

"It does seem like it. If you don't mind, I'd like to just look around the place."

"Sure, man. I'll give you the tour." She slid her feet back into a pair of Nike flip-flops and stood. Apparently, there was no dress code either. "This here's the, I guess you could call it, bullpen." She led him back through a side door and down a hallway. "Here's the kitchen. No one uses it, and the refrigerator smells like death. Bathroom on the right, singular."

The fridge, whew, she was right, he could smell it from where he stood even with the door closed, no janitorial service, he presumed. Assuming from what he had seen thus far, she had few other duties, why had she not cleaned it herself; how could she smell that all day and not?

"If they'd pay me enough, I'd clean it out, but as it is I'm too busy at my desk, know what I mean?" She punched a code into a door and opened it. "Here's the server room."

Harry let out a low whistle, he'd seen and built many server rooms in his time, hospitals, high tech development facilities and even Federal installments. It was not the biggest rack of servers he'd ever seen, but it certainly wasn't the smallest by a long shot. The place was freezing.

He turned back to Meryl. "Lumber company, you say?"

She laughed. "If I were you, I'd come back another time." She locked the door and went back to her desk. "I can take your name and number?"

"No, that's quite all right. Thank you." Harry turned to go but was struck with sudden inspiration. "Meryl. Let's say you were paid to speculate as to what this place is. What would you guess?"

She tapped her lower lip with a badly painted nail. "My money is on gold farming for an online game. Probably through some kind of scam. Set up a simple AI loop, and you can earn virtual 'fake' currency that you turn around and sell for real money. Real cold, hard cash! There's a couple Russians that work here, and they love that shit."

Harry raised an eyebrow. "You know a lot about computers."

"Nah, I'm a gamer. My boyfriend is the computer whiz."

"Speaking of computer whizzes, you got a guy named Calvin Singer that works here?"

For the first time, a shadow of suspicion darkened Meryl's bored face. "Why do you ask?"

"Well, I'm going to be living in the area while this place is getting worked over. I'm from Madison originally and would love nothing more than to settle back down around here. So, I've been shopping and looking at houses in the area, I really liked this particular one on Lake Caroline in Madison county. Turns out it belongs to Calvin Singer, and I have to say he has one of the nicest places I've seen so far. You know his place is on the market, right? I met the guy after hearing about his place from a realtor friend, looked around and fell in love with it. Pretty sure he and I will be making a deal and I hope to be taking it off his hands soon. So really, I was coming up here just as much to shoot the bull with him maybe go grab dinner or a drink since I had to come by anyway, but as I can see, he isn't in."

The answer seemed to generally satisfy Meryl. "Yeah, he says that wife of his just isn't happy living upside other houses, she wants a home in the country, a big one. I haven't seen Cal in forever." She rolled her eyes in disgust. "He was in a good mood last time I did. Said he was going to Atlanta, but he has not answered his phone in months. He sent an email saying not to bother him, guess his wife is wanting some me time with him. And apparently he does almost all his work remotely, but he does get calls to his desk here from time to time. He's got messages, he's got paperwork to sign." She stuck her thumb at the copier over her shoulder. "I've been tempted to call Missing Persons but then, well."

"Well, what?"

She seemed to be chewing her thoughts. "This is weird. They told me not to call the cops, ever. Gave me another number to call instead, said they would take care of it." She sighed. "I'll be honest with you. Whenever you do get a few of them in here, they talk about annoying politics. A lot, I hate politics, don't you, it's always weird stuff about electoral process and stuff like that. If I didn't know better, I'd guess they were trying to hack voting machines. But that's crazy, right? Forget I said that, I'm just venting steam"

Harry nodded, and looked around. "This isn't a lumber company, is it Meryl?"

"Like I said, they don't pay me to ask questions or answer any."

Harry grimaced a bit. Asking questions was pretty much the only thing they were paying him for at this point. He pulled out his tape measure and pretended to measure the wall opening, jotting down notes to be authentic as possible. "Thanks a lot Meryl, I think I've seen enough for now to make my report, you have a nice rest of your day, I'm sure we'll be seeing more of each other soon?"

❋ ❋ ❋

The bar at The Mermaid was about as empty as could be expected, given the it had just opened for the day and the early drinkers hadn't gotten off work just yet. It wasn't the first time he'd been in there, not by a long shot, but it was the first time since he'd come back to see about the house. The bar area had that great aroma of grilled seafood, summer air, and cold beer, almost like being at the beach. It only heightened his desire to stay in the area.

Brian, the head bartender, came by. "What'll it be, big H? Beer or vodka?"

Brian never forgot what a regular patron drank; . Harry was different though; he could never really decide what he wanted till he sat down.

"Crown," Harry said. "It's been one of those days."

"Must have been," Brian said. "You never drink Crown in the summer." He slid over a bar menu.

Harry was waiting for a text. He'd sent a brief message describing, with just enough detail, what was going on up at Revolver. Now he was waiting for an answer so he could make his next move.

One of the things that had surprised Harry the most after he started working for the Company was how little work people like Cal and his friends at Revolver put into not looking suspicious. Spy films would always show multiple layers of concealment. Gleaming office spaces, hidden doorways, everything covered with a veneer of respectability. The reality was often less glamorous. The truth is, people see what they want to, and if they aren't paying attention, it's not only possible but easy for unsavory figures to conduct their business nearly out in the open.

Harry's phone notification buzzed and made a half turn to the right on the granite bar top. He looked down. *Good work. Complete transaction. Will collect package.*

The message didn't sit right with Harry. On the surface, it seemed to be all taken care of. He'd simply hand over a check for the earnest money (funded by the Company and drawn on an unnamed account), sign the paperwork, then wait for the closing. He'd later discuss with his handler about taking over the Southampton place for himself, after it was scrubbed of evidence of course. But his instincts told him something was wrong. Even Meryl, who was nothing if not used to the office being nearly abandoned, thought that Cal was behaving strangely. He was clearly under a great deal of stress, and his last interaction with Harry had been even more off than the previous ones. Maybe something had happened in Atlanta? And was he really planning to deliver his wife to a Southern-belle lifestyle, or was he looking to sell and run before things got worse? Everything about the man was dangerous. He was a time bomb, and Harry was not about to let it go off.

"Anything else I can get you?" Brian asked.

Harry looked up. On a whim, he decided to ask a question. "I'm good, thanks. You know a guy named Cal, comes in here a lot?"

Brian chuckled. "Oh boy, do I know Cal. Why do you ask?"

"I'm buying his house."

"So, he's finally leaving. That wife of his will be happy, I imagine. She's about to drive him nuts, or more nuts. Always going on about getting her some special house."

"What's up with her, anyway?"

Brian looked up and down the nearly empty room. Satisfied that he had time for a chat, he leaned forward over the bar and in a low voice said, "I haven't the faintest idea. All I know is she always orders mint juleps. Every time she comes in, no matter the season. It'll be a week before Thanksgiving, and she's putting back four of them."

"Is she foreign?"

"Russian, I think. Maybe from the Ukraine, street talk has it that she's one of those mail order brides, you know what I mean? She's from one of them Soviet countries, anyway. She's a looker for sure, but every time I see Cal with her, he's scowling. You'd think he could just enjoy it."

"I bet. He told me he'd just come back from Atlanta. Would not be surprised if he's having a little gentleman's time over there. Don't tell him I said that." Harry took a big swallow of his Crown.

"Wouldn't surprise me. He's always going somewhere or another, I think he's going back to Atlanta pretty soon."

Harry put down a nearly empty glass. Brian looked at it.

"You want another one?"

"If you can tell me more about Cal, you bet."

⁂

The neighbor next door was washing his BMW again when Harry rounded the bend on Southampton Circle. He parked his truck on the street and waved to the man, who waved back, friendly and open. He seemed willing to talk, so Harry walked across Cal's lawn and held out a hand.

"Hello there," he said. "I'm Harry O'Keefe. Just bought your neighbor's house. I'll be moving in soon."

The neighbor wiped his palms on his board shorts and warmly, if somewhat wetly shook Harry's outstretched hand. "I'm Bill, Bill Prestige. Welcome to the neighborhood."

"Thanks."

"So, the strange guy is finally moving out, huh?"

"I'm afraid so, and you'll have me to deal with." The men shared a laugh. "Would you really call Cal a strange guy?"

Bill seemed friendly enough, but not forthcoming. He would take some work. "His name is Calvin, isn't it? I haven't spoken to him often enough to even get his name committed, sorry."

"No neighborhood barbecues?"

Bill shrugged. "I'm not terribly active with the neighbors around here. That's more my wife Ann's bag. I just like manicuring my lawn, shining up my little car here, and Mississippi State football; oh, we walk the neighborhood for exercise and wave at the neighbors when we go by but that's about the gist of it."

"Hell of a nice car."

"She's my baby. Ann wasn't too happy about it, but now every weekend she's begging to take her for a ride." He looked over at Harry's truck. "You more of an American engineering fella?"

Harry laughed. "You know, been driving General Motors trucks for a long time, I try to get a new one every three years or so. I've had this one for almost five, and it drives like new. Everyone talks bad about the American auto industry, but GM has never let me down. Had to replace the battery, tires, and some sort of module under the hood but it was covered by warranty; that's about it. Nothing against a zippy little Beemer, you understand."

"Heck, I don't blame you, I had a Ford F-150, all tricked out, but I traded it in for something more fun when I retired."

"Either way, better than Cal's monstrosity." Harry pointed at the orange Hummer sitting in the driveway across the lawn.

Bill shook his head. "I swear, every time he starts that Army tank up it could wake the dead. Who needs a car like that? No gas mileage, isn't even good for hauling."

"It's a toy for guys that like to play soldier."

"You said it." Bill relented slightly. "You know, I've never seen him even at the spring lake social or fireworks on the fourth. And what kind of a guy doesn't like free hamburgers and homemade chocolate cookies, right? He parks that thing in the driveway almost all the time as well. I've wanted to have a chat with him about it—it's an eyesore. But it's his property. What can I do?"

The garage. One of two places where Cal spent all his time.

"You married, Harry?" Bill asked.

"Afraid not, I divorced years ago on account of my 'never rest' work ethic, I guess, and I've been traveling so much; I haven't had much time to devote to a new relationship. Maybe once I get all settled here in Madison, I can start a social life."

"Well, either way, once you get settled in your new place you should come over for dinner some evening. Ann and I would love to get to know you better. I've got to warn you though, she ought to be a private eye." Bill winked. "Nothing much happens on this street she doesn't know about. She's a bit nosy, but I love her."

Harry nodded, trying to focus and not appear rude. But he had a job to do, and he couldn't break his focus. What was Cal hiding in that garage?

* * *

This time it was Cal, not Polina who came to the door when Harry knocked. In fact, Polina was nowhere to be found.

"Oh. Harry," he said. "Wasn't expecting you."

Cal had never looked worse. His shirt hung loose and dirty, and he wasn't wearing socks. He clearly hadn't shaved in days, and there was a worrying smell of scotch hanging around him like a halo. In every way he had the look of a desperate, damaged man. Harry nearly recoiled at the sight of him.

"Cal. How are you holding up?"

Cal gave a bitter smile. "I know how I look. Come in." He waved Harry inside and looked around the whole neighborhood before he closed the door.

The place was in disrepair. The smell left a lot to be desired. Takeout boxes and dirty clothes littered the living room, most of them spilling out of an open and overflowing suitcase. A bottle of whiskey and a Glock pistol sat on the coffee table.

"Polina isn't home, I assume?" Harry asked.

Cal followed Harry's gaze to the weapon on the table. He laughed. "Don't worry. It's not a threat to you. Not even loaded. As for Polina, the bitch flew to New Orleans to see one of her friends. Thank God for small miracles."

Even the tone and tenor of Cal's voice had changed. Whereas once he had put on a smooth Southern drawl, now he brayed in a distinctly coarse Upland South twang. Harry recognized it from the less respectable characters he'd run across in Louisville.

"Have a seat," Cal said. "I insist." He retrieved a water glass from the kitchen and poured a couple fingers of whiskey into it, then held it out to Harry.

"Awful nice of you Cal, but I'm afraid I hit my daily limit at The Mermaid and met a Madison County Mountie on the way over, too. I'm just here to take another quick look around. Gotta drive back, you see. Hope I'm not making a menace of myself coming and looking so often."

"I said, I insist," Cal said. The danger he always threatened was coming forward in his voice.

Harry obliged. He took the glass and sank into one of the love-seats, barely wetting his lips. He loathed the taste of Scotch.

Cal sat across from him with a heaving sigh. "Harry, Harry, Harry. Glad you came by today. Wanted to talk to you anyway."

"Oh? You did?"

"I did, in fact. You know, I'm going to miss this shitty old house. Well, it's not old or shitty. Which is probably why I'm going to miss it." Cal laughed at his own joke without humor. "By the end of the month I'll be out of here. I mean, think about that. How easy it is to just leave a place."

"Well, that's why I'm here this time Cal." Harry sat forward on the cushions. "I was hoping we could move this along. I really want to close this deal as soon as possible. In the next thirty days, if we can."

"Eager to move in, are we?"

"So much you can't believe, I've already started looking at a new pontoon boat."

"Let me tell you what my day's been like, Harry." Cal opened the whiskey bottle and took a swig. "I don't sleep anymore. It's all nightmares. You know how stressful it is to be a cybersecurity expert? You can't imagine it. I get up around noon, I make coffee, pour myself a stiff drink. Try to get some packing done, but that's not happening. And then you come by and brighten me up. Thank you, Harry."

Cal leaned forward and picked up the Glock. He ejected the mag and checked it. Harry saw the bullets.

"Thought it wasn't loaded?"

Cal looked at him. "I saw you across the lawn just now. You getting to know ol' Bill over there? He's a real drag; doesn't drink, washes his car every day and he and his I-spy wife walk the hood almost every day, it's like they never had a worry in the world. Keeps sending notes and calling the homeowner's association, saying he wants me to park my Hummer in the garage. I tell them, I pay the mortgage, I'll park where I damn well please. They send me letters about it, but I just throw 'em in the trash. Can't even remember my name, refers to me as 'that guy at 109 Southampton,' yet he knows to tell me what to do with my life. Just another rich prick looking down on a white trash kid from coal country. Glad to see you two get along so well, though."

The way he held the gun made Harry just as worried that Cal would accidentally shoot himself as intentionally shoot Harry. His blood pressure spiked, and his collar was getting a little wet. "Why don't you put the gun down, Cal?"

"I left something out. About my day, I mean. I'm an idiot. Between pouring myself a drink and taking a massive dump, and well before you arrived. I got a phone call from the office. Sounds like you met Meryl?"

Harry swallowed. "Who? I'm afraid I don't know a Meryl."

"You're telling me you weren't at Revolver today?"

"What's Revolver? You mean like the gun?"

"I haven't answered that phone in weeks. But today, Meryl calls me up. And I answer, good and ready to tell that vape-smokin' little bitch which hole she can shove my messages in. But she cuts me off and tells me some guy came by, asking a lot of questions about me and what I do. Seems to think I work for a Russian online gaming scam, or something. And I hear that, and I remember you coming around, looking at my house. I see you across the street talking to what's his name. And I think to myself, what are the chances this guy's a fucking cop?"

He pointed the Glock at Harry in the most casual way possible, almost as if it was a gag. Harry's mind went blank. This was it, then. Shot to death by a low-level Russian hacker. "Cal, why would cops be poking around your house?"

Cal licked his lips. "You tell me."

"Do you see a psychologist? I don't know you all that well, but I'm very worried about you."

Cal looked down at his hands, first at the liquor bottle, then at the gun. He seemed surprised that he was pointing it at Harry.

"What's wrong with me?" Cal put both gun and whiskey down on the table and buried his head in his hands. "Polina is driving me crazy. She thinks I'm cheating on her. Says, 'Who Naomi? Who Naomi?' Won't listen when I say I'm seeing a shrink. She doesn't believe a big manly guy like me would see a shrink. I've seen some shit, Harry. I've seen and done things no man should ever see or do."

"You mean. In the war?"

Cal looked up at him in terror. "Yes. In the war. I did some awful things to the camel fuckers over there; I know they deserved it. Some people call me a hero, but it don't make it right."

The inflation of his own valor and the edge of racism were enough to finally anger Harry. He wanted to tell Cal that he knew the truth, that the loose tongues around town had revealed his true nature. But he bit it back, remembered why he was there. He leaned forward and put a hand on Cal's wrist.

"Thank you for your service, I really mean that Cal," Harry said. The words burned his mouth.

Cal looked at him through a haze of tears. "You're welcome. I guess. I don't know what to say to that." He sighed and lay down on the couch. "Look. I know I'm losing it. I'll get you those papers as soon as possible. Trust me, if we could close this thing right now I would. You came to look around, look around. Hell, take anything you want. Most of it is Polina's, and she won't be around much longer anyway."

"What's that mean?" Harry asked with alarm.

Cal raised a finger to his lips. "Don't worry, no harm will come to her. She just won't have me to kick around anymore." He rolled over and put his back to Harry.

"Cal?"

A gentle snore came from Cal. Harry shook his head and decided to take advantage of the opportunity provided by his loathsome host's drunkenness.

In the office he found nothing but papers, none of them incriminating. There was a small safe, presumably full of valuable information, but without a way to get in, that didn't matter. What Harry needed was something small, an item that would give the boys in Virginia something to work with. He knew he was outside of his designated task at this point, but with how fast Cal was deteriorating he wasn't about to wait for warrants. Suspicious wasn't the same thing as guilty, and a little data might tip the scale. They could always retroactively make up an excuse for how they got it.

But there wasn't so much as a flash drive, not even in Cal's briefcase. Harry cursed quietly and took a step back toward the den where Cal slept. Then he remembered: the garage.

It was in even worse shape than the rest of the house. It was as if every box had been unpacked, with old magazines, power tools, and random lengths of wire strewn next to broken bird feeders and what looked like part of a horse saddle. This time Harry was going to really look around.

He decided not to bother going through all the assorted junk. Not even Cal was stupid enough to keep valuable information just lying around where anyone could snatch it. No, he liked that fake wall trick.

Harry checked all of them, to no avail. He tapped all over the drywall, listening for a hollow sound, and he felt for joints and seams. Nothing. But then he spied the cabinets. They weren't a likely hiding spot. Unless.

He opened one up and pulled out extension cords, Christmas lights, and yet another bulletproof vest. Harry reached inside and checked the back of the cabinet, and sure enough, there was a seam. He pressed in on it and it popped open like some sort of spring-loaded concealed latch. He pulled it open to expose a secret compartment with a duffel bag inside. He opened the bag and let out a low whistle. Jackpot.

✿ ✿ ✿

Back in his hotel room, Harry flipped open his laptop. He looked down at the flash drives he'd stolen from Cal and allowed himself a wry smile as he popped it into the drive.

There had been two pistols, two boxes of bullets, a combat knife, some instant noodles, an MRE, a bottle of Jameson, four cans of wintergreen-flavored Skoal chewing tobacco, and pile of cash, no less than $150,000 cash he'd guessed, in that duffel bag, most of it tens and twenties, all banded like bank money. Red flags, possibly criminal, but not what Harry needed. Then he found the bag of flash drives, all marked in Russian. Why Cal was storing data on flash drives was beyond Harry, but if he had to guess, they were his master copies. He'd grabbed one at random, praying that Cal wouldn't miss it, stuffed the bag back in the secret compartment, and quietly slipped out of there as Cal laid there on the sofa in a coma-like sleep.

The flash drive contained mostly text files written in what looked like computer code, as well as a few dozen longer documents written in Russian. If this was useful, it would take a translator and a programmer to break it all down, but it seemed like something. That wasn't quite enough for Harry, though. He'd basically defied orders and broken the law to get this stuff, and if he couldn't get something concrete, he'd be fired, or even worse.

"Sneaky bastard," he muttered to himself. He clicked on a document at random.

Well, here was something. It was an email chain in English from the candidate running against the incumbent Senator Armstrong from Georgia. Apparently, if these were to be believed, he'd been collaborating with his party and the local election commission to fix his primary. It was damning stuff, and not the kind of thing anyone would want made public.

Harry wracked his brain for a moment. Hadn't that race taken an odd turn? The whole country had been talking about it, even the folks who didn't live in Georgia. They'd been surprised that anyone would run against Armstrong, a staunch and reliable conservative in a red state. But his opponent had mounted a charge and done good numbers as well. It looked to Harry as if, in his desperation, good old Armstrong had turned to the Russians, who in turn had delivered this compromising material. Or maybe the Russians had tried to fix the race for the other side as well, then turned on their guy and flipped the info to Armstrong?

It would be safe to assume that the other files, the Russian ones, were of a similar nature. Now Harry wished that he'd paid more attention when he'd gotten a crash course in Russian from the boys in Langley, but it was too late for that now. There were plenty of images on the DVD as well, but something told him not to look at those, to ignore them until his nerves were calmer. If they were on a flash drive of blackmail, then he could fill in the rest with his imagination for the moment.

As he browsed, he got a clearer picture of what he was dealing with. He was almost impressed, despite himself. Calvin Singer, proud veteran, had clearly gone a little loose in the head. He had some grudge against his home country and so had decided to put his skills to use on hurting the United States in any way he could. Somehow, he'd fallen upward in Russian espionage organization, probably FSB.

Or maybe it wasn't? Harry struggled to remember. This wasn't his area of expertise. How had they described his mark to him? *Part of an extensive Russian organized crime network.* Well, this wasn't just writing software for some lumber company that doubled as a money-laundering front. This was a lot bigger than all that, but maybe Cal hadn't known. Maybe he'd answered a want ad looking for a security guy at a small local company and then found himself part of something bigger. That didn't explain the Russian wife, though.

All this was far too much to analyze now, so Harry closed the window and clicked on another file. It was a list of some sort, a random series of names with corresponding phone numbers and addresses. Almost all the names sounded typically American. "Anne Shaw," "Jamal Lewis," "Roger McCullough." Although there were some that looked more Eastern European ("Zsigray"), and more than a few that looked like they could be Middle Eastern ("Rizkallah"). There was no rhyme or reason to it, about 250 random entries.

And then, as he scrolled, he saw a line that made his blood freeze.

"Harry O'Keefe," it read, followed by his cell phone number. Well, he'd found something all right.

His phone began to ring. The caller ID showed a blocked number. Harry stared at it as it kept going, unsure of his fate, and unsure of how he'd gotten in this deep.

Thirteen

*T*here had been a lot of shocks in Cal's life. He'd been sucker-punched, fired without warning, locked out of basement apartments where he was only a month behind on rent. Life overall never made a lot sense to him, and things seemed to happen at random for reasons he couldn't discern. It frustrated him to no end, but by the time of his discharge he'd become so used to it that he'd process each shock with a shrug and gritted teeth.

But none of that could have prepared him for the sight of SWAT teams outside the convention center that morning in Atlanta.

It wasn't like Cal was eager to make this trip. In fact, the thought of looking in Adam's lifeless fisheyes filled him with untold dread, but his orders had come directly from Sokolov and there wasn't any way Cal was going to convince the boss man to let him blow this one off. He'd made an appointment to see Naomi the day after, knowing that going back to Atlanta would mess him up even further.

There was no avoiding the trip, though. Cal's plan for escape hinged on Sokolov never suspecting that his son-in-law was planning to disappear in the dead of the night with a pile of cash and a bag of chewing tobacco.

The plan had come together not long after Cal had gotten back to Mississippi after beating that man to death. He'd set up a phony passport, Missouri driver's license, and paid in cash for a one-month stay at a cabin on the Mexican border. He had a buyer for the Hummer in Houston. And he'd already found a used car on Craigslist, and after that his trail would go cold. He'd cross over into Mexico, blow some of his money on cocaine and pretty women, then move on till he got to Brazil. Maybe become a bouncer at some sleepy tourist trap on the beach. Cal would cease to exist.

He was looking forward to it, too. No more nagging wife, no more psychopathic Russians threatening to kill him on a weekly basis. Just good weather, cold beer, and a fantastic exchange rate.

The plan was so simple, it kind of shocked him when he put it together. For a while, stricken with nightmares and deeply depressed, he'd tried adding all kinds of stuff to it. Spending more time in the U.S. to throw off the feds, buying a plane ticket to Thailand. He even considered killing Polina, both out of spite and fear that she would rat him out, before he thought better of it. Abandoning Sokolov's daughter would surely infuriate him but murdering her would bring down a storm of violent fury far beyond what running away would justify.

Cal felt blessed that the feds weren't onto him, at least not yet. The big threat would come from Sokolov and his endless, shadowy network of proxies, operatives, and government functionaries, all of whom were so tangentially related to the central Sokolov enterprise and obscured from each other that it was impossible to know when and where his boys would show up to torment Cal. His research had shown him that Brazil was likely far away enough from the sphere of Sokolov's influence to make finding Cal difficult. Sokolov was into buying and selling elections in the United States, and his Russian counterparts were far more interested in the Middle East and Central Asia than they were in South America. They wouldn't waste their time on little old Cal.

The most important thing about the whole plan was selling the house. Sokolov hadn't given Cal a raise in quite some time and Polina's ravenous spending was burning through his Revolver paycheck like there was no tomorrow, leaving precious little in the way of savings. Cal had squirreled away what he could and hidden it in cash, but the bulk of the funds for his great escape would have to come from closing the deal on the house and withdrawing all that money. Without it, he'd be staring down the barrel of poverty again. He wasn't sure when he'd get the chance to work again, and there wouldn't be many chances for him to peddle his skills as a cybersecurity expert going forward.

Harry was the wild card. This guy had come out of nowhere and provided a solution to a problem that hadn't even reared its head yet, like a mild-mannered guardian angel. Cal liked him as soon as they met. A little anxious, but also super friendly and apparently guileless. But then he'd seen Harry talking to what's his name next door. For a full twenty-four hours Cal contemplated tracking down Harry and shooting him in the head. What if the guy wasn't just a construction manager looking to settle down but was really a cop or, worse, CIA? What if he'd been stalking Cal from the very moment he set foot on that plane to Russia? The illegal nature of Cal's work wasn't hard to discern, and further-more, anyone who set foot inside the Revolver offices would be able to see it wasn't really an office but just a big front for a mass identity-theft scam. And now of course, some very valuable infor-mation on voting habits in the state of Georgia.

But Cal pushed that thought out of his mind; he was becom-ing paranoid in the aftermath of the beating in Atlanta, when in reality his position with Sokolov was more secure than it had ever been. If anything, they had more incentive to hide Cal from the authorities, now that he was more intertwined with the organiza-tion than ever before. He was becoming, if not indispensable, then a very valuable asset to the operation.

Which is why it was such a shock for Cal to pull to the curb across the street from that convention center and see it surrounded by police officers. He'd been banking on this going smoothly. He'd meet up with Adam, do the handoff, maybe have a little small talk and ask if he'd done any interesting killings recently, then fly back to Jackson. The Atlanta trip was supposed to be perfunctory, something loathsome but necessary so as not to arouse suspicion. It was not supposed to be a giant shitshow.

Cal peered around the building from the street. A crowd of rubberneckers had already formed, and a whole lane of traf-fic was being redirected. There were no signs of fire or violence from the outside, and the police officers milling around out front didn't seem like they were in an alert mode. Their calm demeanor clashed with the heavy armor and rifles they carried with them.

The effect was one of total control and domination. They had achieved victory, and from here it was all paperwork.

Cal got out of his airport rental car and ambled over to the crowd near the police tape. He shoved his way through until he came across one of the officers. "Afternoon, sir. Any idea what's going on here?"

The police officer had on a large pair of mirrored aviator sunglasses and a stern demeanor. "Please stay behind the line."

"Oh, of course. I was just wondering. Looks like a heap of trouble, doesn't it, somebody rob the place of something?"

The officer grunted. "I'd say it is. You with the press, trying to get an interview or what?"

"More like just a concerned tourist from Louisville, curious about what's going on like all these other folks, that's all, sir."

"There was a disturbance in the penthouse. That's all we can say right now; you'll have to watch the six o'clock news for the rest."

Ice shot through Cal's veins, and he somehow managed to sweat even more than he had in the Georgia heat.

The police officer eyed him with suspicion. "You got any other business here, buddy? You rubber-necker's are all alike."

"No," Cal said quietly. He backed away and shoved through the crowd, half running back to his rental, desperate to get away before suspicion fell upon him. Maybe it already had, and there was nothing he could possibly do after all. But he'd be damned if he was going to wait here for them.

✿✿✿

Harry spent the entire night before on the phone with his handler back in Langley. Since signing on, he had wanted to get involved in a high-profile mission; this was his first case. To him, he'd hit the jackpot of cases to be a lead investigator on. His performance on this one would increase his personal stock value, add to his performance history and very well land him an offer of a an even higher profile case not to mention that he could demand a higher fee. If he could crack the case, pull off the arrest and get his hands on all the documents to make it stick, it was almost guaranteed.

Harry had begun to take a liking to Cal, to him, Cal was a victim of circumstance brought on by his Russian father-in-law. He had formulated several scenarios where he thought, with a little finesse, he could get Cal a deal if he'd come clean and maybe even get Cal off or at least a reduced sentence if it went to trial. This was mind boggling, Harry was a green horn independent contractor but this was far more exciting than any high-rise topping-out party that he had ever been a part of in his former occupation. Harry wanted to go public with what he'd found, leak the documents to the press, blow the whole thing wide open. The way he saw it, this was an enormous miscarriage of justice. If American lawmakers, more than a couple of them, were employing Russian mob hackers to get an edge in their elections, that would be the biggest scandal in modern history. It would upend everything about how elections would be handled moving forward. Hell, it might even lead to a new Cold War, but it wasn't as if somebody in Russia didn't think the first one was still going on. This needed to be made public.

"Can you imagine how people would respond if they knew all this?" Harry had said.

"That's exactly why you're not going to say word one," his handler had said. Her voice was clipped and tired, but mostly firm. "This stays between us, understand. It's above your pay grade as it is. If you were an official part of the agency, I'd already have you reprimanded for sticking your nose in this."

"And I'm glad that I'm not. But if you'll forgive me for being frank, this sticks at the heart of what makes us who we are. It wouldn't be right not to say something."

"This is an internal matter. We'll be arresting those responsible, and we'll be creating new protocols."

Harry had begun scrolling through the files again as he spoke. He stopped at a particularly damning image of what looked like some real estate developer. "I took a look at the photos."

"Dammit, I told you not to."

"I don't think a few revised protocols are going to cover it."

"What people do in private is their business."

"I agree, but once you start trading materials like this for money it stops being private. This is a disgrace, and one that must be brought out into the open. Sure, a few people will lose their seats, maybe some of them will be locked up. But they absolutely deserve to be."

"Do you think this is the first time something like this has happened?" An edge of anger crept into the handler's voice. "Every once in a while, some foreign entity decides they want to meddle, and every time we put them down. Those responsible are quietly dealt with, and they're never seen alive in this country again."

"With all due respect, I don't think you understand the scope of this."

"What do you mean?"

"Well, everyone mentioned here is from the region south of the Ohio River and east of the Mississippi. So, what about California? How about Vermont, or Michigan? I doubt Cal is the only one working for these people. He doesn't seem that bright. What if you don't get everyone involved in this scheme?"

"We don't fail."

"And what happens when they keep it up? What if next time it's a general election, and they decide who sits in the Oval Office? What happens when they have compromising material on the sitting president, and he or she has to sit behind that desk deciding where to send our troops, knowing that if they do something the Russians aren't pleased with, they can say goodbye to their entire career? That's not a decision they should have to make. That's not a country I want to live in. That's not my America."

"But it is your country Harry. I love this place more than you can imagine. I've spilled blood for my flag, and I'll do it again if I have to."

Harry shook his head. "It's not right, I tell you. The people of this country have a right to know."

"That's not for you to decide, you know this already, why are you persisting like this, you need to settle down Harry."

Harry sighed. Well, there was no convincing her. "Then what do I do?"

"Finally, you ask the right question. I need you to coordinate with your man Belvedresi, down there. He needs a warrant so they can search that house and get the wife. I also need you to figure out if he's spoken to anyone else, and if so, I need you to bring them in for questioning."

"And Calvin? What about him?"

"Why do you care? Do you feel sympathy for a traitor, come on Harry, don't go soft on me this early in our relationship, it's not becoming of you?"

"No, not exactly. But he seems like he's had a rough time. I want him stopped, more than anything. I'd just rather this happen with as little bloodshed as possible."

"He'll be in Atlanta tomorrow. We'll get him there."

❀ ❀ ❀

It was well after midnight, and Cal was still sitting in the hotel bar chasing shots of Jameson with Budweiser. He drank robotically, not tasting the stuff, and seemingly not becoming more inebriated either. It was a dark and twisted ritual. It was the last meal of a dying man.

Cal had been texting, calling, and emailing everyone he could think of for hours. The others in the network, his counterparts to the west and east; they said nothing. Neither did Adam. He'd called Sokolov only to find that the number was disconnected. That wasn't odd: his father-in-law was constantly ditching cell phones. What was odd was that Cal hadn't been given the new number.

He didn't want to admit it, but this wasn't just about a lock-down. It would be one thing to go radio silent in the aftermath of a disaster. Keeping communications to a minimum made sense. What didn't make sense was not giving instructions to the bag-man and security expert who was currently married to the boss's daughter. It only meant one thing: Cal was the one taking the fall for this.

He knew he should be on his way back home already, that he should be grabbing his stashed go bag and booking it for the bor-der. But for some reason, Cal couldn't bring himself to escape. Maybe it was because he still held out hope, his thoughts drifted to Polina, what was she up to in his absence, was she waiting patiently for him at home with her nighty and all smiles, he thought Not, was she secretly packing the car and headed to parts unknown? After all, it had taken several hours and numerous ignored calls for him to begin to come to terms with the situation he found himself in. There was still a limited chance that it was all a big misunder-standing, and he'd be summoned to a more secure location. Adam would take the bags with a dead smile and shake his hand, and they'd all be on their way.

Cal waved down the bartender. "Another round."

The bartender looked at the empty glasses in front of him. "Last call is real soon, and you've had a lot mister."

"And I ain't going anywhere. So, pour me a drink and let me wallow in it all."

The bartender shrugged and poured him another double scotch and refilled his mug from the Shock-Top tap. For some rea-son, Cal thought back to the last drink he shared with Matt and laughed. He hadn't thought of Matt, not anymore, not for a long time. If he'd spent any time at all considering the first casualty of his new career, he'd have quit years ago. And now he was in the same spot, with a bunch of Russians currently looking to hunt him down and extract what they needed. Well, he'd be damned before that happened.

Cal downed the round of drinks, then another. He threw down some bills at random, way too much money, but he didn't care at that point. He stumbled up to his room, dumping the computer bag with the hard drive in it in one of the corners as he slammed the room door closed. Cal had a premonition of trouble on this trip, so he had declared a handgun in his checked baggage in Jackson. He pulled the handgun he'd stuck into his belt and put it under the pillows, checking for the millionth time that it was loaded before flopping down face first on the mattress.

He thought of Kentucky, the gentle hills and hazy blue skies, the lowland horizon of forests and corn fields. He could remember the smell of his mother's cigarettes on their back porch in the lazy summer afternoons as she sipped hot black coffee and said it made her cooler than sweet tea for some reason, and the way his tennis shoes would stick to the linoleum at his high school. At one point he had just been a boy, somebody's son. Shooting hoops with his teenage buddies on Saturday and pooling their change for a milkshake at Sol's on the corner of Main and Third downtown; life was so simple then, he thought. He smiled as he wondered what might have happened to the long rope swing, they used to swing out over the flooded borrow pit near the river where they'd skinny dipped. Even the girls would swim with their panties and bras on while the guys stared in hopes of seeing something exciting. Why was life so complicated and hard now? He felt all his life that he'd been destined for nothing much of anything, but now at least he had the right to die in peace, or at least in glorious battle. But all that had been taken away from him. Or maybe he'd taken it away from himself, when he'd refused to act right. It wasn't like the world had ever given him much reason to, yet if he'd known he'd wind up here there's no question that Cal would have done something, anything different. If only to alleviate the enormous and nonspecific sense of dread that soaked him to the skin and ran outward, infecting everything.

❀ ❀ ❀

Naomi was wearing a plaid flannel suit today. She crossed her legs and frowned. "So, you're not here for therapy?"

Harry settled back in his chair and shook his head. "I'm afraid not. Not that I'd mind having someone friendly listen to my grievances for a couple hours. But I'm actually here because I need to speak to you about one of your patients."

"Well, I'm sorry to tell you Mr. O'Keefe, but I'm not at liberty to discuss any of my clients or patients, as you call them. Unless of course, it's a matter of them harming themselves, or others. So, it looks like you wasted your time."

Harry nodded. "And under any other circumstance, I would respect that. But what if I told you this is a matter of life and death? Or even more, a matter of national security?"

Naomi leaned forward and lowered her voice. "Are you … hearing voices?"

"Only when I'm on the telephone," Harry chuckled. "Sorry. Bad joke. I'm here because I think that Calvin Singer is a threat to the United States and the citizens around him, and I'm wondering if you can give me any insight into that."

"I'm sorry, Harry, but you know the rules surely, I can't give out information on my clients."

"Are you telling me there's been nothing? No suspicion that he isn't who he says he is, or that he's far more dangerous than he claims to be?"

A flicker of recognition crossed Naomi's face, and she looked down at her own crossed fingers.

Harry sighed and reached into the inside breast pocket of his blazer, pulled out his State Department ID and handed it to her. "Naomi, I promise I wouldn't be here, asking you to do this if it wasn't of the utmost importance. You can call Chief Eddie Belvedresi with the Madison County Sheriff's Department. I'll wait. He and I go way back, and he knows I'm here. And you can call the sheriff himself, and you can get the local FBI on the phone as well. They know there's been somebody poking around down here. I'm that somebody. And I just want to close this all up, before Cal does something drastic."

Naomi stared down at the ID for a long time. It identified Harry as a contractor, but it wasn't like those operating at the behest of the CIA would have that on their papers anyway. Harry worried that he was outing himself a bit, but he felt more comfortable getting her to speak on her own than detaining and interrogating her.

Finally, Naomi spoke without looking up, not much more than a whisper. "You think he might have killed someone?"

"I don't know, and it's not my place to speculate. But if it was, I'd say that's quite likely."

"He's quite the liar," she said. "I don't think he's so much of a hero as he's made out to be."

"Now, listen here Naomi. I've got an unmarked car out there with two officers who are more than happy to escort you some-where safe so we can have a chat. I don't think it'll be much of a violation if you tell us about this lying, cheating murderer who's been coming to see you. What do you say to that?"

She took her time answering. Seemed like it was more about shock than any kind of moral conflict. But finally, she looked Harry in the eye and nodded.

❖ ❖ ❖

The knock on the hotel room door was enough to wake Cal up, it sounded more like somebody beating on the door with their fist. Cal pushed himself up and he sat on the edge of the bed; he looked down in disgust. He'd vomited in the night; it was all over his shirt sleeve and on the front of his shirt; the comforter was ruined. He stood up with a short stagger and wiped his mouth as the knock came again, louder this time. Cal stared at the red numbers on the bedside clock it was 11:30 a.m. already, who in the hell is at the door, he thought.

"Mr. Singer?" a masculine voice he thought he recognized came through the door. "This is the hotel manager. It's past your checkout time. We need you to leave immediately."

His head was pounding, and his eyes watering, but Calvin knew enough to recognize that this was it. He didn't believe for a second that it was the hotel manager knocking. He retrieved the pistol from under his pillow and crouched behind the bi-fold closet door near the bed, waiting for the inevitable.

There was another knock and then some low swearing. "Mr. Singer, I know you're in there. You don't have to go home but you can't stay here."

Cal didn't say anything. He just crouched, tense, ready.

"Maybe he snuck out. Hang on, let me get the key."

The card went into the lock and clicked, and the hotel room door gradually opened. A man Cal didn't recognize slowly edged his way in, clutching a gun in his left hand. Another followed him and bringing up the rear was none other than Adam.

"What tha hell," one of them said. "Smells like death in here, what is that?"

Adam picked up the laptop bag. "He's hiding. I told Sokolov he was a coward."

Cal's anger spiked, and he popped out from behind the door, gun outstretched, and opened fire. One of the thugs caught two in the stomach and the other caught three in the chest and one in the shoulder. They went down faster than Cal expected.

Adam dropped the bag and pulled out a pistol. Cal ducked just in time, punching out his empty mag and shoving in another. His military instincts kicked in and he rolled away as the rounds tore through the mattress. He popped up and fired twice. One bullet

229

clipped Adam's gun arm. The other hit him in the throat. The room turned deftly silent.

His heart pounding, Cal crept over, heart pounding so loud he could hear it. Adam's blood spilled out over the carpet as he scrabbled at the wound with his good arm, his eyes pleading with Cal to do something.

Cal picked up the bag, slowly. He slid the gun into it and looked Adam in the eye. "It's what you deserve, you sadist son of a bitch."

Hatred filled his eyes, followed by fear. Then nothing at all.

Adam's phone rang, and Cal bent down and picked it up.

"Da," said his father-in-law, followed by a string of angry Russian.

"I thought we had something special, Dad," Cal said, cutting Sokolov off. In his adrenaline-filled state his sense of humor had returned.

There was silence for half a minute, before Sokolov spoke again. "Stay away from my daughter. I do not want her around for this."

Cal laughed. "It's my house, you bastard. It's always been my house. If she wants to live in my house, then she can deal with me."

"She has left you Calvin Singer, this no longer concerns her, you will never see her again." The line went dead.

Cal retched and spat. There would be time for fear and panic later. He ran to the window and thanked whatever god there was that it was a second-floor room. He leapt down and cursed as soon as he hit the ground, but there was no time to address the sharp pain in his ankle. He half ran, half limped to his rental and tore ass to the airport, he had just 20 minutes to return the car and board his one-hour flight back to Jackson.

It wasn't the smartest thing to be doing eighty through town, but Cal was having a hard time balancing his fear of being caught with his need to get away, besides, he was barely keeping up with the other traffic. The plan would have to change. He needed to tell someone, because there was no longer any chance of him escaping unnoticed. Even if the feds were clueless as to the true nature of Revolver, they wouldn't be able to ignore three dead men in his hotel room. There had to be someone who would listen to him. Harry wouldn't. Hell, they just met. Polina was gone, having finally abandoned him to likely sun herself at some beach near Miami, he presumed.

Finally, a name appeared to him: Naomi; he was scheduled to see her today anyway. He pushed the accelerator to the floor, his teeth set, determined to pull this through. He would have to wipe his pistol of prints and stuff it in a garbage can somewhere before he got to the security pass-through.

✿ ✿ ✿

Cal screeched to a stop outside the mental health clinic and ran inside, tucking the pistol he kept under the seat of his Hummer into the back of his jeans. He pushed past families, orderlies, and right up to the reception desk.

"Naomi? I need to see Naomi. Now. It's urgent."

The receptionist was taken back, but it was clear that she dealt with distressed individuals on a regular basis. "I'm terribly sorry, sir," she said in a quiet tone. "But it seems that Naomi isn't here right now."

231

Cal stared. His skull felt empty, and his heart pounded. "I don't get it, it's the middle of the afternoon. How can she be out? This is an emergency, you understand. I'm one of her patients and I need to see her now."

"If you're distressed, we can have someone else speak to you. Or we can call 911 for you."

"No! Don't even think about it. I need to talk to her now, you hear me."

"Sir—"

Rage coursed through Cal, like no rage he'd ever known. It was beyond any of his fights, beyond his hatred of Polina, and well beyond even the fury that had driven him to break that pretty-boy Army officer's arm. He pulled the gun out of his pants and pointed it at the receptionist.

"You bring me Naomi," he said, quietly. "Get on that phone and find her and tell her to get her ass back here. Now, you hear me woman. Or I'll blow your fucking head off."

The receptionist yelped and put her hands up. Tears started in her eyes. "Sir, please. Please don't do this. Put the gun down."

For a moment, something like remorse came to Cal. But then it was washed over in another wave of anger. Who did this bitch think she was, telling him what to do?

He didn't even realize the gun went off. Cal just heard a loud bang, and the next thing he knew the receptionist was on the ground, clutching her side, screaming in pain and fear.

There was shouting behind him and Cal whirled around. One of the other patients, a burly guy in overalls, charged at him. Cal fired wildly and the guy stopped short and stumbled, clutching his knee.

Cal pointed the gun at the terrified people around him, one after another. To let them know that he wasn't to be trifled with, that he was in no mood for shenanigans. He backed out of the place slowly, wordlessly, all the way back to his car. He hopped inside and sped back to Lake Caroline.

***

Cal backed his Hummer up to the garage door as it opened, and quickly leaped out to raise the rear hatch door. He went in through the front door because his instincts were still functional. The Russian guy in a suit who was waiting in the kitchen didn't even have time to pull his piece before Cal shot him in the back. The poor bastard had expected him to come in through the garage, like he usually did, but Cal was smart even in his panic. In fact, he felt alive in a way he never had before. In some way, this was his true nature. Him against the world, fighting to survive. Well, it wouldn't be the first time. He kicked the man's corpse as he went out to the garage.

Cal had a hell of a time popping the back of the garage cabinet so he could get his go bag. It was almost as if someone had put it back up in a big rush, but that was impossible. Who would come for his bag? Nobody knew about all the secret compartments he'd built into this place. He'd done it himself, over Polina's long weekend trips to go spend more of his money with her idiot friends in Florida. Cal had been industrious, opening up walls and sectioning off spaces to hide the materials he needed to survive.

He finally popped it and wrenched the bag open. His heart damn near stopped. The money was gone, and so were all the flash drives full of sensitive data, the backups he'd made and received that he'd packed in case he got desperate and needed blackmail, or to sell to some South American cartel. In fact, the whole bag was empty save the scotch, the wintergreen Skoal, and a single pistol.

There was a note in there too. It just said, *I'm sorry, you have killed our love, Polina.*

Love. What a fucking joke.

Cal shook his head and laughed. He laughed longer and louder than he had in years, and when he was done, he cracked open the bottle of Jameson and took a big pull. He grabbed a can of Skoal and popped it open, putting a big plug in his bottom lip. As he passed through the kitchen, he grabbed a coffee mug to spit in. He walked through the house full of hideous furniture and grotesque wallpaper into his office, where he pulled down the wall behind the closet and methodically, patiently, loaded up his favorite rifle, a Colt M16 fully automatic and stuffed a thirty-round magazine in each back pocket. He began grabbing all his weapons and moving them into the back of his Hummer. He knew he had to move quickly, surely the cops were on to him and would be there at any moment.

Fourteen

Shortly after Harry first arrived at the scene, he had offered to draw a floor plan of the house to indicate, as best he could, where he remembered Cal had stashed weapons and ammunition; the location where Cal was most likely to hole up in. It was so hot that he had to start over several times as the sweat from his forehead continued to pour onto the paper and foil his drawing. Each time Deputy Sandridge's radio would squelch, it would cause Harry to lose track of where he was on the paper. Finally, he finished and handed it to his friend.

Sandridge looked at Harry's sketch of the house. "Well, that should do it all right, if it comes down to us storming the place."

"I've got to be honest with you, I'm thinking it will," Harry said. "I just don't see this guy coming out of his own free will. His therapist agrees."

"What has she been filling his head with? Can't have been much of a therapist if this is the kind of results she gets. Good Lord."

Harry's phone rang, and he stepped away. The caller ID said, "Bluelite."

"I got something else for you," said Bluelite. "It ain't for their ears, because I shouldn't even know about this, but it looks like your boy in there left three men dead in a hotel in Atlanta."

"You mean the one they put on lockdown? If he was in there, what's he doing here?"

"Well that's the thing, Harry, he wasn't in that hotel. This was one on the very outskirts of town, some busted-down motor lodge with the world's dirtiest bar attached to it. And one of these guys, Adam, last name Ostelot. Seems he runs that business you had me look up, Revolver or whatever."

"Well, I'll be damn, really?"

"Dammit Harry, you told me this was all going to go down in Atlanta. You said you'd get your man and buy your house, and we wouldn't have to hear any more of it. So why is there a half-crazy disgraced soldier emptying rounds into my squad cars?"

Harry was silent for a while. It did seem like he'd made an error in judgment here. It would have been simple enough; warn the Atlanta PD of the situation, work with them to shut down the convention center hotel where a lot of Cal's noise kept going to, and pick up the suspect while he was there, selling to the Russians. Except there had been an error, one even the eggheads in Langley hadn't seen.

"Eddie, look, I'm really sorry about all of this, man, I mean I never wanted to put you in a situation like the one we're in now, I wanted to stop him, not set him off."

"Well, you have not succeeded."

"I'm thinking, our boy here didn't sell to the Russians, I'm thinking our boy worked for the Russians, and when Atlanta's finest stepped off that elevator, they realized they had a leak. There was no alternative spot to do their drop. The Russians thought they'd cut him off."

Eddie was silent for a second or two. "I assume what you just speculated to me is above my security clearance?"

"Come on, Eddie. I've known you how long? You know I wouldn't knowingly get you in any kind of trouble."

"You don't call this trouble? Well, I ain't making any promises about saving that house of yours, you know."

"Yeah, I had a feeling."

✤ ✤ ✤

At that moment, the biggest issue for Cal to deal with was his bleeding arm and the dwindling booze supply. He'd managed to wrap his forearm with a kitchen dish towel to stop the bleeding, but it had been three hours since he'd started exchanging rounds with the Sheriff's Department, and in that time, he'd dipped his way through a whole can of Skoal, drank most of the bottle of Jameson and bled out a bit. All that was left in the house was some fancy vodka Polina favored and some schnapps. Cal grabbed a nearby door facing and swung his head from side to side. He felt weak, apparently having lost enough blood and thinned what he had left down with alcohol, so much so that he was getting lightheaded. He grunted and tightened his stomach muscles as if to shake it off; he could not let this take him down, he thought.

Normally Cal didn't think of himself as much of a drinker. It was more of a casual thing for him, a purely social affair. Sure, he could put it back when the moment required, but before Atlanta he wasn't going through bottles at a time. Of course, once the nightmares set in, that changed, and he became the kind of guy who could have a fifth to himself. In any case, he had no intentions of dying sober or passing out and waking up in a prison hospital.

Dying? The thought terrified him, at this point it seemed likely that there was no chance of him surviving the encounter. Those cops wouldn't have been happy to see him when they found out he shot a woman; let alone the two cops he'd winged since this started. In fact, it seemed the only reason they hadn't stormed the place as it was because they'd intuited that he had enough guns and ammo to take on the whole department. He adjusted the body armor he'd strapped to his chest and tightened the rag tourniquet. Seemed like the Madison County sheriff wasn't interested in making sacrifices, and that didn't surprise Cal. Most people didn't know what it meant to sacrifice, to risk your life just to get a little bit further ahead. They weren't willing to go all the way.

He briefly considered what would happen if he gave himself up. Assuming they didn't riddle him with bullets the second he stepped outside, they'd arrest him, charge him, convict him and put him away for life or worse. Forget about the three dead men in Atlanta and forget about the wounded in Mississippi. Cal was guilty of treason, and maybe even eligible for the death penalty. He could get that infamous cocktail shot in the arm. But even if they gave him life, that wasn't any kind of life at all. Sure, he could fight. But Cal knew it would only be a matter of time before one of Sokolov's guys took him down. How is that any way to spend one's last days? He'd be looking over his shoulder in a federal maximum-security facility, waiting for someone to slip a knife between his ribs. No, this was better.

The home phone rang again. The first couple times Cal had answered, it had been some asshole cop, trying to offer him money and a way out like he was stupid. No way there were letting him walk a free man. It was obvious that the police weren't entirely sure what they were dealing with. Cal kept waiting for the FBI or worse to call him, someone who understood that he was a low-level technician for an ex-KGB crime lord working at the behest of Putin's Russia. Maybe that guy, the mysterious agent, could help unravel the web of Sokolov's empire. Cal would like to know before he kicked the bucket.

The phone rang once more, but not the landline. It was his cellphone, still running on about 20 percent battery; the name surprised him, it was Harry.

Cal cleared his throat and took a swig for courage. He answered the call and put on his most jovial voice. "How's it going, Harry?"

"Well, Cal, not too good." Harry said. "Not good at all."

"Oh no? I'm sorry to hear that, is something wrong?"

"It seems like the previous owner of my house has holed himself up in there, and the Madison County Sheriff's Department is having one hell of a time getting him out."

"You don't say, that's strange, isn't it? What's this world coming to? These kids, they just can't seem to do right. Always carrying on and getting into trouble, sticking their nose where it don't belong and then acting all surprised when they get bit."

"I'd say that about covers it."

"Funny you should mention all this, as a coincidence, it turns out I'm involved in a kind of shootout with the police right now, myself."

They both laughed, it was good to have a little levity.

"You watching this shitshow on television?" Cal asked.

"No, as a matter of fact I'm right outside."

Cal poked his head up, just enough to peek, moving any at all made his arm start bleeding again. He couldn't see Harry, but that was his voice, he was certain of that.

"No way. Hope none of these rounds came your way. I wouldn't want to hit you." And to his surprise Cal realized that he meant it.

"There have been some close calls, I'm afraid."

Cal got serious. "You really ought to get out of there, Harry. They'll come by to collect what's left of me and clean the place up in the morning, I promise you that."

"You see, Cal, I can't leave right now, the Sheriff's Department asked me to be here, special, just for you. I was up on the hill, out of harm's way, but they thought maybe it best if I came down and you and I had a little chat. We'd all really rather not have to come in there and bring you out in a body bag."

So that was it, something about this, maybe the gentle tone, maybe the casual wording. confirmed Cal's suspicions. But he wasn't angry, just mildly amused. "How long did you know I was a traitorous dog, Harry?"

"Well, I wouldn't use those words, Cal. I think you're hurting awfully bad, and you might have gotten in a little too deep. I'm thinking the boys back at the Company might be able to do something for you though. Why don't you put your guns down and come on out here where we can talk?"

There was silence for a minute as some scrap of information floated up from the depths of Cal's mind. "The Company," Cal said quietly to himself, "is how agents of the Central Intelligence Agency refer to their place of work when around civilians. Do you work for the CIA, Harry?"

Another pause, even longer. "You know I couldn't answer that even if I wanted to, Cal. Now come on, you got every chance to do right, here. You got a head full of knowledge, and there's somebody just aching to get at it. It doesn't have to be prison, Cal, at least not prison the way you're thinking of it."

Cal leaned back against the wall, phone to his ear; the offer was tempting, then again, it also seemed like it could be some kind of bluff. Harry didn't look like what he expected an agent to look like, but then again maybe that would make him a better agent. Well, it didn't matter now, even if he was, he was just trying to get ahead like Cal was. They probably paid those guys better than they did the soldiers anyway.

"Let me call you back, Harry," and hung up the phone.

❊ ❊ ❊

The next couple hours were mostly silent. There were a few bullets exchanged, but at that point Cal was just stalling so he could think.

241

He hadn't really liked to think, up till that point in his life. That's why he hated school so much, all the thinking they wanted him to do. What good was any of that? None of it was going to serve him in the long run. But now, with nothing but time on his hands, he didn't see any reason not to sit down and have a think, and maybe figure out how he got here.

I think you're hurting awfully bad. That's what Harry had said to him over the cellphone. Cal had never thought about it in those terms. He'd thought of himself, more or less, as the victim of unfortunate circumstance, a man who might have done better in a different time. He was all grit and rage, and that wouldn't do in a world that expected you to stand up straight and shut your mouth. And perhaps, in some way, it could be said that all those accumulated feelings were Cal hurting awfully bad.

He was more used to thinking of himself as hurting others and never anyone that didn't deserve it. It was always someone that sassed him or didn't appreciate him. When not that, then it was some guy with an attitude problem that needed some adjustment. Up until that man in Atlanta, Cal thought of himself as a righteous avenger. But he didn't know who that guy was. Adam had never once told him what transgression he'd performed to deserve being beaten to death by a stranger. Now Adam himself lay dead on a slab in the morgue, he deserved it for sure. But did the two who came in with him, guns pointed? Did that receptionist in the clinic, or the guy that had tried to stop him? How was Cal any different from a crazed gunman?

Cal's eyes welled up; his site nearly blinded by the gush of tears. No one would miss him, once he was gone. His family, what was left of them didn't know if he was alive as it was; his wife had finally given up on him. The closest thing he had to friends were Brian at The Mermaid and Harry, some nobody who had come by to buy his house and sell him out to the feds.

A bit of his old fury came back to him. He could punish all of them, take out a whole bunch of these pricks. Load up the grenade launcher and rain down anarchy. Go full Rambo and finally get the bloody satisfaction he'd so craved for years. Wasn't like there was a God for him to disappoint, and even if there was, Cal wasn't on his way to any kind of eternal reward. He could go down in a blaze of glory the likes the state of Mississippi had never seen before. He'd be immortalized in sacred flame.

But did they deserve it? That was the question. Did he deserve revenge against the whole world? Was it all right for him to kill without remorse, to inflict punishment on the country that had rejected him? Harry's voice, kind and warm, still hung in his ears. That man didn't hold any ill will toward Cal. Traitor and murderer though Cal was, Harry still recognized his basic humanity. Well, Cal didn't feel very human, but he didn't want to disappoint the only person who still believed in him. And maybe he could atone in some small way.

Cal dialed Harry's number and listened to the ring. It was soothing.

"Hello, this is Harry O'Keefe," said the voice on the other end, as if there was any question.

"There's a safe in my office," Cal said, quietly. "The guy I work for is named Sokolov, he's based out of a town called Breznygrad in the Moscow oblast. I don't know the extent of his organization, but it ain't small. You're going to want to raid Revolver as well. My wife is somewhere in Florida, I believe, maybe Miami and she's got most of the good shit. There's some in the safe, but not a lot."

"Thank you, Cal."

"The government of the U.S. might be nothing but sons of bitches all the way down. But the biggest bastards I ever met were these Russians, and they deserve whatever hell you deliver."

"That's right, Cal, that's good, now you come out my friend and we can talk a bit more."

"Well, that's the thing, I'm coming out, but I ain't coming peaceful. So, if they want to live, they need to leave or come in now."

"Don't do this Cal, I'm telling you, there's all kinds of concessions that can be made for you. I don't want to be disdainful, but you're pretty small fry in the scheme of things; we're trying to catch bigger fish; you could help us do that Cal."

Cal laughed. "Thanks, Harry, that's what I needed to hear, nothing like a bit of encouragement at my lowest moment in life. Take care of yourself man, enjoy the house and do something about these repulsive curtains, won't you?"

Cal hung up and drained what was left in the Jameson bottle. With his good arm, he drew himself across the bedroom floor and into the master bath. He pulled himself over into the spa tub, laid his pistol in his lap and rested his M16 on the edge of the tub, believing for a fleeting moment, that he could stand them all off and escape in the dark. His arm began to bleed profusely, the make-shift tourniquet was no longer holding it back and the room had begun to spin like a top. Cal had been lying, of course; just like always, he wasn't going to hurt anyone ever again.

The grenades came through the windows, trailing white smoke; tear gas, it immediately set Cal to coughing, as chemical tears streamed down his face and mixed with the real ones. He could see the bedroom wall from his position, one of Polina's disgusting tapestries sparked and broke into flames. Fitting, he'd really loved her one point, but that time was gone. To Polina, Cal was just another image in her dream of an American life as a kept woman. She was the last thing he thought of as he raised the pistol to his head and squeezed the trigger.

EPILOGUE

The fire and water damage were extensive by the time they got the place under control. Deputies and investigators had to worked by floodlight, deep into the night and into rising dawn, looking for some rhyme or reason for this tragic and hostile incident. The spa tub in the master bath held his body along with his fully automatic M16, 750 rounds of 5.56 mm full-metal jacket ammunition and Cal's Glock 40-caliber. His body lay in a pool of his own blood that had leaked from his arm from the single wound inflicted by one of the deputies in the earlier skirmish. The fire hadn't spread far enough to reach Cal's remains, but the heat and smoke made for quite a mess when they zipped him up and got him out of there.

Bluelite came through later to assess the scene, shaking his head as he went. He'd never seen anything like that in all his years, and he made sure everyone knew it too.

He clapped a hand on Harry's shoulder. "Shame about the house, I did the best I could."

It really was, to Harry anyway, he really liked the place, and it would have made a nice little bonus to the long and difficult process of bringing Cal in. Most of the structure still stood of course; it was just that a lot of the interior was burned to hell and the rest was black from the heavy smoke that had filled the entire house.

"She'll be all right," Harry said. "I've seen worse brought back to life, someone will live here again, I guarantee it, just time and money, that all she needs."

"Maybe you?" Bluelite said. "It'll take some work, but I'm sure you can make something out of it."

Harry didn't answer, he crossed the lawn and went inside, picking his way past firefighters. They looked at him as if to warn him not to come in, but after the long ordeal no one was looking to talk more than they had to. He made his way to the office. It wasn't as badly burned as he expected, but the fire had made its way back there. On what had been the floor was a safe, badly melted and opened. Somehow Cal having a cheap safe made a lot of sense. The documents inside were mostly charred, useless. From what Harry could tell, it was mostly Cal's personal papers: birth certificate, passport. There was some sort of contract written partially in Russian that might have been useful if it wasn't so burnt.

At the bottom of the stack was a photograph of a few teenage boys. One of them was unmistakably Cal. Tall, lanky, tow-headed, clearly a mid-schooler in the middle of a growth spurt. Their shirts said *1992 Owensboro Middle School Spring Break*, and behind them was a lake, with boats on it and a long rope hanging over the water from the bough of a large oak tree. He looked happy in a way Harry had never seen him. He tucked the photo into his pocket and walked back onto the lawn.

"Find what you're looking for?" asked Bluelite.

"Yeah," Harry said.

He turned his back to the house and looked toward east, the sun was just now throwing up a lighter blue over the horizon, oblivious to the sins that had taken place below. Harry had originally purchased the place on the government's dime for the sole purpose of this investigation but now that they'd have no use for it, it would very likely be put up on government surplus property auction. He truly loved the place and was hopeful that once the boys back at Langley were done sifting through it, he might cut a personal deal for it, as-is, or at least make the successful bid offer when it came up; after all its what Cal would have wanted.

ABOUT THE AUTHOR

HARVEY GREEN was born and reared on a large cotton plantation in the rural Delta, outside Clarksdale, Mississippi. After graduating Mississippi Delta Community College with an Associate Degree in Construction Science, he worked as a construction executive and cost estimator with a major commercial construction firm for more than forty years. He currently lives in Madison, Mississippi, with his wife Judy, has two children and currently five grandchildren. *Nobody's Patriot* is his debut novel.

CPSIA information can be obtained
at www.ICGtesting.com
Printed in the USA
LVHW030758111119
636963LV00001B/155

9 781733 757751